The New World

The New World

by
Louise Michel

translated, annotated and introduced by
Brian Stableford

A Black Coat Press Book

ISBN 978-1-61227-117-0. First Printing. October 2012. Published by Black Coat Press, an imprint of Hollywood Comics.com, LLC, P.O. Box 17270, Encino, CA 91416. All rights reserved. Except for review purposes, no part of this book may be reproduced or transmitted in any form or by any means, electronic or mechanical, including photocopying, recording, or by any information storage and retrieval system, without permission in writing from the publisher. The stories and characters depicted in this novel are entirely fictional. Printed in the United States of America.

Introduction

Le Nouveau monde by Louise Michel, here translated as *The New World*, was originally published by Dentu in 1888. It is a sequel to *Les Microbes humains* (1887)[1] and was intended, when it was prepared for publication, to be the second in a series of six books, although none of the others were ever written.

Michel informed journalists in 1887 that the titles of the other four books would be *La Débâcle, ou le Cauchemar de la vie* [The Debacle; or, The Nightmare of Life], *Première Étape* [First Stage], *L'Épopée, ou la légende nouvelle* [The Epic; or, The New Legend] and *D'Astre en astre* [From Star to Star]. One periodical, the *Gazette anecdotique*, reported that the author was "correcting the proofs" of all five of the volumes intended to follow *Les Microbes humains*, but this was wildly optimistic. In fact, there is strong evidence that the proofs of *Le Nouveau monde* were never corrected, any more than the proofs of *Les Microbes humains* had been. The published volume contains a plethora of inconsistencies and errors of the same kinds as its predecessor: names are routinely misrendered, and are often given in several different versions, sometimes within the same chapter; sentences are often run together, and sometimes arbitrarily split up by paragraph breaks.

The nature of these errors suggests strongly that the copyist who produced the text from which the typesetter

---

[1] Also available in a Black Coat Press edition as *The Human Microbes,* ISBN 978-1-61227-116-3.

worked, or the typesetter, if he was working from an autograph manuscript, could not read the author's handwriting or follow her punctuation. While improvising as best he could, the typesetter presumably expected these errors to be corrected before publication, but they were not. Michel's failure to correct the proofs of *Les Microbes humains* might have been due to the fact that she was in jail for much of the latter part of 1887, and, by the same token, her failure to correct the proofs of *Le Nouveau monde* might have been due to the fact that she was shot in the head in 1888, when an unsuccessful attempt was made to assassinate her. At any rate, the job was evidently not done, and the published text of *Le Nouveau monde* is a worse mess than that of *Les Microbes humains*, frequently becoming incoherent and sometimes incomprehensible.

The coherency of the existing text is not assisted by the manner in which it was composed. *Les Microbes humains* is something of a patchwork; two other stories, presumably written some time before the main narrative, are inserted into the main narrative, one of them seemingly as an afterthought rather than being added to the main narrative while it was in progress and thus integrated into it. Although that is one of the least satisfactory aspects of the earlier volume, Michel obviously found the strategy convenient, because the main narrative of *Le Nouveaux monde* similarly absorbs at least one pre-existent work while in progress, and is then supplemented by half a dozen more, four of which are simply tacked on to the end when the main narrative has petered out, with only the most tokenistic attempts being made to connect them to that narrative.

It is possible that all except one of the parts making up the patchwork text of *Le Nouveau monde* existed in some form before the author received the long jail sentence that prompted her to write her memoirs and the principal narrative of *Les Microbes humains*. Having had the first volume accepted for publication, she apparently set out to revise the earlier materials, recomplicating the plot of the main narrative by introducing one quite different story as a subplot, but it appears that the effort in question began to falter about half way through the present text, when the main narrative loses all impetus, limping on thereafter to a direly unsatisfactory conclusion, padded out in the meantime and afterwards by various other texts, only one of which appears to have been finished in its original version. Weary of the labor, or distracted by other things, the author stopped doing any substantial revision about two-thirds of the way through the text, her efforts thereafter being minimal, and the novel dissolves into chaos—a unfortunate fate for a book written by one of the most famous Anarchists in the world, who spent her later life fighting against the popular misconception that Anarchism = anarchy = chaos.

Like many writers whose method is simply to make up their plots as they go, Michel seems rarely to have reached the end of any of her fictional projects, and never to have been able to contrive any sort of satisfactory narrative closure. That is probably why she postponed the conclusion of her overarching scheme until a much later volume than any she was ever likely to get around to writing, even if she had managed to continue the series into a third volume. Thanks to her list of prospective titles, however, and the passages inserted into *Le Nouveau monde* advertizing the continuation of the story, we do know what that scheme was to have involved. The third volume would have featured a worldwide catastrophe, geological as well as political, whose survivors, guided by the superhuman scientist Dr. Gaël and the messianic Josiah, would have established a new Anarchist society, all of whose members would have been physically transformed into potential immortals; in the meantime, their communication with the people of Mars would have provided the foundation for an interplanetary community of Anarchist societies.

Lovers of science fiction are bound to regret that the later volumes only ever existed as extravagant ideas in the author's head, although they would doubtless have observed that all the narrative energy and drive of the first two volumes comes from their representations of the dire iniquities of the existing world, and that nothing survives of that energy and drive the moment the story attempts to move beyond horror in the direction of hope. The exceptional nature of *Les Microbes humains* lies in its representations of evil: the general evil of a legal system that routinely lets the guilty go free while punishing he innocent severely, and the particular evil of utterly corrupt and vicious villains who commit or collaborate in serial murder—sociopaths, in today's terminology. Michel was obviously aware of that, and made advance preparation to supply the projected third volume of her series with a new pair of villains to replace those featured in *Le Nouveau monde*. That problem is, however, endemic to popular fiction in general and futuristic fiction in particular; devoid of active human malice or, at the very least, of catastrophic human tragedy, it tends to become bland. The penetrative element of narrative is active or tacit evil; in its absence, there is no story but only style.

In the event, not only did the series briefly anticipated by its author fade into oblivion, but *Le Nouveau monde* fares no better in itself. It is, in effect, a novel that might have been rather than one that actually is, and although the appended stories are not entirely without interest, they are a poor substitute for a genuine denouement to the main narrative, which remains sadly devoid of any kind of climax. In view of that, *Le Nouveau monde* is mainly of historical interest, and would not have much of that had it not been the work of such an intriguing historical figure. If it had not borne the signature of Louise Michel it would never have been published, and no one would be interested in reading it; the fact remains however, that it *was* written by Louise Michel, and it does offer a useful insight into her worldview and way of thinking that is not contained in any of her non-fictional writings.

Michel was not the only leading Anarchist to dabble in writing thrillers. Her sometime collaborator Émile Gautier also did so, in the short scientific romance "Le Desiré" (1892) and the long novel *Fleur-de-Bagne* (1902; co-signed by and presumably ghost-written for the ex-chief of the Sûreté, Marie-François Goron),[2] but not until abandoning political activity; Jules Lermina also made a living as a writer of popular fiction, and so did Henri Ner, alias Han Ryner. None of the others, however, contrived anything like the raw defiance of Michel's fiction, and all of them were, in effect, following her lead—including Lermina, who was nine years her junior but launched his literary career much earlier. Her work is, therefore, of historical interest in the context of literary history as well as political history.

---

[2] To be published by Black Coat Press under the title *Spawn of the Penitentiary*; I have already translated samples of relevant work by Jules Lermina and "Han Ryner."

This translation has been made from the London Library's copy of the Dentu edition of *Le Nouveau monde*. I have unified the rendering of names that are given in several different versions in the original, and have corrected numerous proper names—adding explanatory footnotes to problematic instances—but I have simply left out a few presumably-misrendered names whose actual referents I was unable to ascertain, and which were irrelevant to the text. The author's extensive use of argot would have been problematic even if the typesetter had not misrendered many of the argot terms, and in several cases I have simply had to deduce intended meanings from context. I have made corrections where there were obvious typographical errors and manifest errors in punctuation and syntax, and have done my best to extract what I believe to have been the intended meaning from numerous incoherent passages; inevitably, I have probably made some mistakes in the latter process, for which I can only apologize.

Brian Stableford

THE NEW WORLD

Preface

Here comes the Red Easter![3] says Jacques' song: the Red Easter when the human chrysalid, tearing its envelope, will open its wings wide in the breath of summit. It senses the free air. Here it comes, solicited by the light, sensing new aptitudes.

The ideas that have germinated in the shadows are developing, lucid and triumphant; one sees beneath their true daylight that things that the darkness made vague and deceitful.

Justice, so long nailed down in human jails, science and the arts, all those rudiments that have always been stifled, have come to life, and the new legend passing through the epic will be magnificent in its growth, which is the law of progress; all the nations having become humankind, all our dialects having collapsed into the universal language.

Only a short time separates us from that dawn, but the setting sun is so somber and the ruins of the old world, circled by the crows, so horrible that many people deny tomorrow's light.

People thus denied, before the invention of the telescope, the infinity of worlds gravitating in space; before

---

[3] Actually, Jacques song, as quoted in the text, refers to the *coq rouge* [red cock] rather than the *rouge pâques* [Red Easter], but the metaphorical import is much the same.

the microscope, the world in a water-drop full of monsters. In the same way, the blind would deny colors if other eyes than theirs were not open to the light. Can we see distinctly, through the holes in our charnel-house, liberated humankind on the liberated Earth?

The first part of this book, The Desperate, is the nightmare of life; in the second, some of those desperate individuals attempt to live as they think people will live in the future. Who can say that they are wrong? The third is the destruction of the new colony by the civilized people of the old world.

The next volume will describe the cyclones, the collapse of races, continents and ideas, and the possible emergence of the dream of the new legend.

I. The Nightmare of Life

How many people, in our centuries-long autumn, throw away the cup that is still full, not wanting to drink the disgust of life therefrom?

Children, old people and the young go thus into the shadow from which no one returns. Many, ground down, fight among themselves, holding one another responsible for the common distress. Have you ever seen flocks at the doors of abattoirs thrashing about madly while awaiting the slaughter whose odor envelops them? In a similar human confusion, the new world is fermenting.

For a long time—forever—that is the way it has been.

In this book, we are digging in a corner of the charnel-house.

Under the arches of the railway between Levallois and Clichy, on one of those spring nights when the mild and heavy darkness is like the wing of a nocturnal bird, two men are finishing their horrible work in profound peace.

A third, lying at their feet, is no more than an inert mass, like a pole-axed ox.

One of the men commands the other: "Undress him! Put the clothes in this suitcase."

The other lifts up the corpse and strips it.

The body, still warm, is supple, the task easy; but those movements have reanimated the unfortunate victim; his breast rises, breath escaping in a rattle from his throat.

In the distance, the cracked voice of one of those daughters of misery who are known as "good-time girls"

rises up, mingled with the vague croaking of the drunkard who is with her:

> Beauties, beauties
> Are faithful to gold,
> Lan laire, lan lin!
> The juice of the vine
> Makes the face red
> In drunkenness![4]

The murderer drops the body, which renders a last
plaint. The girl and the drunkard sing:

> Beauty, beauty,
> Come and have a chat!

"Quickly!" says the man in command to the other,
lifting up the suitcase in which the clothes have been
heaped with one hand, and putting a knife into the
wretch's hand with the other.

The latter, who had reached out to receive payment,
shivers, and his teeth chatter.

"Cut his throat!" says the master.

The other bends down without replying. Is it not
necessary to go all the way to the end? Stupid as the man
who sells himself may be, the bargain must be completed; the wretch whose flesh is creeping must go on, must
go on to the end.

The knife is blunt; it's necessary to put pressure on
the throat. The victim twitches again.

---

[4] Like all the other songs cited in the text, this one is rhymed
in the original, but I have translated the meanings directly
without attempting to reproduce the rhyme-schemes.

Close by, the drunk and the girl sing:

The earth is reeling
Open a full barrel!

The final word catches like a cry in the throat of the man and the cracked cooing of the woman. Nothing more.

The body writhes in a pool of blood, springing like a fountain from his open throat.

The blood has splashed the murderer's face. In his overly large shoes, his bare feet have been wetted. A tremor shakes him, however, the man whose throat has been cut is no more than a cadaver. The silence is profound.

It's not over.

The man giving directions with calm imperturbability hands the other an enormous stone.

"Crush the face!"

He obeys again. The bones of the face crack like a nutshell. Who, now, would recognize the cadaver?

This time, the master pays. The two men separate.

One, suitcase in hand, his pace steady, goes toward the Avenue de Clichy, the beginning of the lighted quarters; the other, trembling beneath the rags that would leave him naked but for the night, which dresses him in shadow, plunges into the road to the fortifications, He stops at one of the dilapidated huts facing the bank.

In the hut, the silence is so great that no one would suspect the presence of living beings.

The man gropes in the shadows. Are they asleep? Are they dead?

He tries to speak, his voice choked by the horror in the depths of his throat, escapes in sobs.

"Marthe! Marthe!"

It is so strangled, that voice, and so terrifying, that the woman utters a cry; he does not hear it.

"Marthe! Is the little one dead?"

"No!"

The man breathes in deeply.

"Where is he?"

"Here; I'm warming him up; he isn't crying any longer."

"I have the money."

"You haven't killed someone?"

"Shut up—we have to save the child."

His wife stifles a groan.

"Courage! You have to live. A little wine will warm him up."

He puts his hands on the child's body and feels that it its icy.

"Hold him close to you—I'll go fetch the wine."

A tavern not far away is showing a sliver of light.

The man knocks on the door.

"The child's ill!" he shouts. "I need wine—good wine. Open up, Monsieur Nemo. The kid might die."

"Who's there?"

"Me, Pierre."

No reply.

Pierre knocks again.

"Open up! I've got money."

At that assurance, the door opens.

The lamp, shining in the face of the man who comes in, displays his blood-spattered rags in all their horror. His shoes have left bloody footprints on the ground.

Seeing himself, he tries to run away, but the tavern-keeper, and strong and swift as a guard-dog, bars his way. Two agents who are drinking there, waiting for daylight, leap on to his shoulders.

Thinking about the dying child, he shakes them off as a wild boar shakes off the dogs, knocking them over, and, grabbing a bottle placed on the table, flees before his adversaries, rudely thrown to the ground, have been able to get up.

This wine, he thought, is the child's life.

The agents, hurt by their fall, had scarcely regained their feet when Pierre had already got back to his house.

"Quickly, Marthe! Make the child drink!"

The chills would never drink again; he was dead.

The hut was so full of shadows that they could not tell exactly how the misfortune had occurred.

"No light! No light!" they said, madly.

It was the agents, guided by Monsieur Nemo, who were bringing a light.

The tavern-keeper knew where his client, who had been insolvent since illness had caused him to lose his job, was living.

The unfortunates did not try to resist. The child was dead; there was nothing more for them to do in the world.

The paltry face of the little creature was livid, his body already stiff; he was definitely dead.

That little one was the last of the brood; the other three had perished by virtue of going to work too young; it was for him that the father had committed murder.

They let the mother lay him down in his crib.

We too, she thought, grimly, *are going to die!*

And like wolves caught in a trap, the man and the woman marched away in silence.

Another nest had fallen from the tree of poverty—but many still remain on its branches, waiting for the new spring.

II. The Man with Bright Eyes

While his accomplice was being arrested, the man who had supervised the murder continued slowly and placidly on his way toward the heart of Paris, suitcase in hand.

Near the Place Clichy, at a display-window that was still illuminated, there was a man as thin as a stray dog, draped in a blouse that had become too large, falling from his shoulders in elegant folds. Glued to the window, his face hollowed by eyes lit up by hunger and thirst, he seemed made of stone; the anxiety of his features revealed a terrible suffering and an intense energy.

Momentarily, the man with the suitcase considered the man glued to their window, between the sinister glow of a street-light and the faded illumination of the café; then, going over to him, he placed a hand on his shoulder. It was either the caprice or necessity of having a docile individual in hand, or to establish a current of public opinion in case his crime became known.

"You're thirsty, eh, comrade?"

The other, raising his head, only made out the vague outline of his interlocutor, a shadow floating like a lost thought. In the grip of hunger, the somber visage had, as if through the holes of a mask, two eyes as phosphorescent as those of a wolf: two bright eyes, like lamps.

When the hungry man did not reply, the man with the suitcase repeated: "You're thirsty, eh?"

"What's that to do with you?"

"You're in a bad mood. Me, I'm a maniac; I like to save people who are drowning, in life or the river. I save them whether they like it or not!"

"You're crazy. Leave me alone."

"No. I sold a painting yesterday. You're an artist, I can see that. We'll share it. I have a thousand francs on me; here's five hundred."

He put a fistful of gold coins into the hungry man's hand and drew away, looking back to see what the other would do.

The unfortunate's first impulse was to throw the money in the face of the overly generous unknown man, but the second was the instinct of a thirsty beast; he ran into the café. *I'm dreaming*, he said to himself, *but before I wake up, I need a drink!*

That's good, thought the other as he moved on. *He's caught in the trap*.

"Drink!" shouted the starveling, sitting down at a table. It seemed to him that he could drink a whole barrel, a glass as big as the great vat of Heidelberg,[5] or the Ocean. Eyes dilated and mouth open, he repeated: "Drink! Drink!"

One of the gold coins he was holding rolled on to the floor tiles as he set the others down in front of him on the table, where they slid with a slight tinkling sound.

The man would surely have committed a murder for less—perhaps several.

The café had stayed open during the night because of a local festival. Night-birds, newspaper-sellers and street-performers could drink there. Agents, "patriotic sharks" and "bottom-feeders," came there in disguise to

---

[5] A big barrel, said to be able to contain 200,000 liters of wine.

watch one another. Strange things were heard there, sinister and burlesque.

In one corner, two old men are "having a few jars."

A young coxcomb sitting between two slutty tarts is oiling them up.

At the far end of the bar, a peasant from the Haut-Marne, arrived in Paris that day to buy a trousseau for his eldest, Rose, is sitting between two of his daughters. After several circuits of the fair, he is letting them rest in the café.

An old man, parceled up like a winter onion, is feeding drinks to a little girl who still has an ingenuous expression, in spite of everything.

"Another glass, Mionette?"

In a voice that makes argot sound sad, she replies: "Yes, another, always. Perhaps I'll find you less nauseating when the booze has tangled my bobbin."

She's right, the poor girl, for it's a horrible pendant that the imbecile has just picked up for a night at the fortune-teller's—but her purse is empty and the beautiful girl is full of sap, and has to live! It's necessary to follow the same road as the rest, damn it, since she has to live and hasn't the means. There is, however, something in her that is in revolt; there are children of both sexes who, seeing the whole of life before them like a cut throat, don't want to enter upon it and kill themselves on the threshold.

"Drink!" cried the thirsty man again, having absorbed all the liquids set before him. Then, another draught having been poured, he raises it to his lips and falls under the table.

"It's not worth the trouble of falling over," said one of the agents, observing the singular drinker. "It won't save him." Calmly, they lift up the human mass inert on the tiles.

A few gold coins were missing at the count; they were only able to confiscate two hundred, without knowing where the rest of the Eldorado had gone.

The Haut-Marnais was long gone, a daughter under each arm.

All the others watched. Passing in front of the café, one dragging the other, were a half-sobered-up drunk and a thin creature in rags, floating like feathers. That skylark of poverty was La Greluchette,[6] the girl who had been singing in the dark alleyway of the fortifications.

---

[6] *Greluchette* means "lover," in a contemptuous fashion.

III. An Essay on Wolves

Bestial characteristics are not so extensively modified in the human animal that they do not reappear, often with frightening energy; one cannot say that they have been effaced in anyone, since our societies conserve them with the struggle for existence between individuals, not in communal conquests of the forces of nature.

The man with the bright eyes—the eyes of a wolf—who directed the crime in the first chapter, was one of those rare bestial specimens complicated by various anomalies. In him, exaggerated faculties of instinct disputed with an enormous idealism. There was an eternal conflict within him between the human and the bestial, the monster sometimes succumbing and sometimes rearing up again, avidly, like the vulture of Prometheus, the human being bound to that torture.

Such was this product of our troubled era: a strange product, which the circumstances of birth, education and environment had combined to infantilize.

He had something of the physique of double monsters, Siamese twins like Millie Christine[7] and others, connected by membranes. It was by intelligence that the man with bright eyes was bound to his twin brother. A current of electricity enveloped them, rendering their passions, ideas and maladies common, like monsters attached to one another by sentiment and instinct.

---

[7] Millie and Christine McCoy, born in 1851, became the world's most famous conjoined twins, exhibited by several different showmen, initially in rather unsavory circumstances. They were usually billed as "the two-headed nightingale."

23

The mother of the Wolff twins, an orphan of a family of financiers, had been able to indulge her fantasies; she was passionate about hunting; first her guardian and then her husband obtained equal pleasure from that pastime.

One day, contrary to her habit, she went astray in the paths in the wood. Night fell without her being able to rejoin the other hunters. She let her weary horse move on at a placid gait, and, no longer able to hear the horn or the dogs, took an avenue that went through the woods. Slowly, she was going back to the lodge, dreaming about the son to whom she would soon give birth, when her horse baulked and snorted, reluctant to go on. A black mass flowed, splitting and doubling, drawing along four lights as bright as stars.

The huntress bravely fired the two shots from her light carbine at the group.

The four lights went out; she had hit two wolves that had been fighting one another, each full in the head.

The lady had been fortunate in aiming at the lights; she had shot two wolves of enormous size.

The entire hunt emerged noisily into the clearing, searching for her by torchlight. There were immense acclamations; the enormous bodies of the wolves, lying beside one another, were visible in the torchlight.

A few months later, the lady gave birth to two twins, so perfectly similar that even their mother could not tell them apart.

Hazard marked one of them in an indelible fashion.

Baron Wolff had thrown a party to celebrate their birth, concluded by fireworks. The château caught fire. The twins were carried out in haste.

One of the infants, dropped by his nurse, fell on to a copper frame heated by the fire; there remained on his arm a Hebrew letter, ר, the *reich*,[8] the first letter of the name of the great ancestor Roll.[9] From that moment on, the twins could be distinguished from one another, and the name of Roll was given to the one who bore the letter.

No mother was ever prouder than theirs—they were intelligent and beautiful—but none was more sorely tested either, for, at the back of her mind the memory remained of the mysterious terror of the night in the wood. Leaning over her sons' crib, she rediscovered, disturbingly, the bright light of wolves' eyes in their pupils; even their hair, wild and bushy, did not grow in silky curls like that of other children, but remained short and coarse.

Sometimes, a anxiety gripped the poor woman; her sons' twinkling eyes—their beautiful eyes, which she called her stars, but which, in the depths of her heart, troubled her with a vague terror—did not fix themselves upon her for long.

Baroness Wolff died of languor; the rich have that leisure. From then on, the children, more frequently in the company of an old domestic, Étienne, than that of the Baron, gave evidence of penchants that frightened the old retainer.

---

[8] The Hebrew letter in question is nowadays usually rendered as *resh,* but I have retained the original's spelling.

[9] The reference to "the great ancestor" suggests that this name should really be rendered either Rollo or Rolf, with reference to the Viking settler Hrolf, who was the ancestor of the Dukes of Normandy and once laid siege to Paris. The latter's name is nowadays commonly rendered in either form, but never as "Roll."

Their play, in which white teeth drew drops of blood from pink flesh, alarmed the old man. It contributed to their hasty separation. The twins were not put back into the same crib.

A common upbringing should have sufficed to make them forget their antipathy, like cats and birds reared in the same household, which sleep side by side; prudent human stupidity had the contrary effect. To crown the work, an uncle in the Antilles, who was devoid of an heir, simplified paternal surveillance by taking one of the terrible brats to live with him.

Lots were drawn; chance, which definitely had its eye on Roll, designated him for the voyage.

Between the ages of ten and twelve, the uncle brought him back to spend a few months with his family. The twins greeted one another with a grinding of teeth dissimulated by education. The hatred was no less keen, increased by imbecile precautions and undeniable fatalities.

After their meeting, Roll and Philippe conserved that strange hatred, perhaps originating from the impression experienced by their mother, coldly and implacably; they detested one another; others might have been epileptic.

An event modified the character of Philippe. He married for love—a rare thing in the rich caste. The wolf evolved then. New strings vibrated in his breast, and the sheep, black or otherwise, that hazard threw beneath his judge's paws received less harsh treatment. The proud and gentle Anna enveloped him with tenderness. She alone had awakened the human being.

Roll, on the contrary, in the hot climate of the Antilles, felt his hatred of Philippe increase. It infiltrated his blood to the point of insanity. To live his brother's life, to gnaw him like a worm, to annihilate him—to eat him, if one might express it thus—was his ardent desire, so avid was Roll's hunger.

On learning about Philippe's marriage, his obsession became more intense. He wanted his brother's wife, as he wanted everything that belonged to him. Was not his brother the cause of the exile in which he had been brought up? It was an exile overflowing with wealth, but which had nevertheless had that effect on Roll's thinking.

The near-simultaneous death of the father in France and the uncle in the Antilles permitted Roll to put into action a plan that had been ripening for ten years. He liquidated his assets and took passage on the whaling-ship the *Whole*,[10] which had called in at the Antilles on its way back to Europe.

Not far from the Brest Channel, the *Whole* suddenly sank beneath the waves. The ship was heavily laden; the passage is perilous and the catastrophe seemed to be natural.

The *Whole* had, it was said, perished with all hands and cargo, but not all of those who are never seen again are dead. Philippe was wrong to wear mourning for his brother so light-heartedly.

In order to realize his obsession, Roll needed to be believed dead. He brought his enterprise to a successful

---

[10] I have left the name of this ship unchanged, although subsequent revelations confirm that it is the same whaling vessel named—rather unimaginatively—as the *Whale* in *Les Microbes humains*. The chronology of the present text, although confused, is difficult to reconcile with that identification, and the account of the ship's sinking given in this volume contradicts the one given in the earlier book.

conclusion. The loss of the ship did not appear to him to be too great a sacrifice to ensure his safety. Henceforth, Roll Wolff the planter no longer existed. He was about to become Philippe Wolff, the famous magistrate charged with the most arduous investigations. His studies and his perfect resemblance to his brother permitted that.

Whichever of the two Martin Guerres[11] was the false one had a thousand times more risks to run than Roll Wolff. Once the crime was committed, however, he was not unaware of certain difficulties—the petty details of his brother's life were unknown to him; fait might have surprises in store for him—but there is a arrogance that suspicion cannot reach. He was counting on that.

---

[11] The case of Martin Guerre in the mid-16th century became legendary; it involved a probable imposture, complicated by the fact that the missing Martin's wife initially identified the substitute as her husband, but changed her mind after another man, ultimately judged to be the real Martin Guerre, turned up.

IV. An Artist's Dreams

Jacques the sculptor was asleep, as he had not slept for a long time; his bed had a mattress, sheets and a coverlet. How had all that come back from the pawnshop? Jacques was no longer hungry; a powerful sap was circulating in his veins; that reparative sleep was really doing him good.

Lying there half-awake, in the benevolent morning warmth, he heard vague whispering; someone was talking about his work—the group of the future—and he was afraid of waking up completely.

"It will be a sensation," someone said, "an enormous sensation."

That swarm of people in a narrow space! It's marvelous! The judges have been impressed by it.

What judges? Has his work be accepted, then? Jacques had been working on that group for two years.

The future in progress! An entire human phase, following an idea, hands raised toward a light.

The flames twist; one can see them radiating, throwing off sparks; the group is buoyed up by the rhythm of the new epic, passing through the ruins, over the cadavers of the past. The idea emerges from the symbolic group, grabs you, gives you a frisson of future things, for which our rudimentary languages lack words.

Thus Jacques saw his work during the two years that people spat at it and he defended it.

Now it is admired, he examines it for faults; he searches it. "It's beautiful!" people say. No! It's a coarse sketch, a heap of pretentious stones; those who whistled it were right. The group is not upraised, borne upwards by a vertiginous course; its tread is stupidly measured. The breathless torsos, the avid mouths—none of that is rendered; there's no life in it. It's a failure! It's dead!

He is disgusted by it. What? That's what cost him so much work; it was for that that he stayed up late and went hungry for two years!

Those nations which, holding one another by the hand, surround the group, like the hours around the chariot of the dawn, now seem to him more wretched than a circle of waltzers; everything that he thought expressive is mute; it's not even a sepulcher; it's mute.

Why did he bother, anyway? Can one do anything before the evolution of humankind? Then, that of which he dreamed will be the real art, will have another ideal; it is always thus in endless progress. What develops in the full sun of liberty will be the gilded fruits of the centuries-long summer; we ourselves are hasty fruits pricked by worms, which nevertheless give a foretaste of those of summer.

Jacques' thoughts went so far through the phases of humankind that they became lost there, flapping our heavy air with their open wings; he was far away in that warm atmosphere, allowing his thoughts to fly toward the unknown dawn.

A noise at the door made him raise his head.

It must be Madame Gachette, the concierge, who has come to bring Jacques his morning coffee. He knew full well why Madame Gachette had given up that habit, but he was unclear as to why she had resumed it.

"But that's my kind Madame Gachette," said the artist, almost regretting waking up.

It was not Madame Gachette bringing his morning coffee; it was a prison warder, who deposited a tin-plate mess-tin containing the morning soup on the shelf beneath the peephole of the door. The group had disappeared with the visions of the dream, and there was no bay window open to the air but a barred slit in a narrow cell.

Jacques was in jail. That was why he had a mattress on his bed.

What the Devil had he done, and why wasn't he hungry anymore?

The gold of the man with bright eyes had brought the starveling bad luck.

Who wouldn't have arrested him? Drinking avidly, as if he wanted to forget some crime, with gold running through his hands on to the floor...

Jacques was in solitary confinement; his case seemed to be linked to that of the unfortunates from the hovel. Three of the murderers were thus in the power of the law. As for the victim on display in the morgue, no one could recognize the completely-crushed face. They were reduced too suppositions.

Hands of considerable delicacy, in spite of the breadth of the palm, indicated that the man belonged to the class that does no manual labor; that explained the gold that had come into the possession of the murderers.

The investigation of the mysterious affair was entrusted to Philippe Wolff. Things could not have worked out better; his luck was complete.

V. Martin Guerre

If Roll, dressed in his brother's clothes, had presented himself to anyone who knew the latter, no one would have doubted that he really was Philippe. Both of them had such dark complexions that the climate had only been able to add an imperceptible difference when one saw them together.

The magistrate's wife, rendered anxious by her husband's prolonged absence, waited for him with her children asleep in her lap. The room in which she was sitting, containing the children's beds, was very much the red and ermine nest of the children of a judge, who sits in a red robe, with ermine on his shoulders.

Roll would not have chosen differently.

Philippe's wolf-cubs, still sweet beneath the blond hair that they got from their mother, along with their father's bright eyes, were savage and charming: wolves crossed with a lioness, thanks to their mother.

Those innocents had neither the mind nor the character of their race; thanks to their education, they would only have the intelligence. Tall and strong for their age—they were between four and five years old—they had never left their mother as yet, incessantly enveloped by her skirts, playing or running around her. She loved them dearly, the poor things.

The old domestic Étienne, whose features Roll recalled vaguely from his early infancy, had never left Philippe; Roll required, at that first test, as much cleverness, and perspicacity extended to the point of divination, as the greatest geniuses put into their work—

perhaps more, the instinct of self-preservation mingling therewith in all its intensity.

The old man shivered at the sight of Roll. *That's death passing by*, he thought. Poor old faithful dog that he was, he scented the wolf.

Roll, giving the excuse that he had work to do, shut himself in his brother's study, where he spent the rest of the night going through correspondence, files and intimate letters. He entered into Philippe's life.

In the morning, he went to his wife's apartment. She too had stayed up late. The children had been afraid; she had only just got them to sleep. Her blonde hair covered the pillow like an unbound hayrick. She was truly beautiful, Philippe's wife, and Roll felt his bright eyes fill with flames as he looked at her.

A reflection made him smile. *What the Devil is her name?* he thought.

Raising his eyes toward an escutcheon embroidered on the curtains, he saw two names interlaced: Philippe and Anna.

V. Lost Children

The night is black; it's raining; a horse collapses on the shiny roadway. In spite of blows, the animal remains on the ground; it can do no more. Pedestrians break into a trot or lengthen their stride, according to the length of their legs.

It's late, and the rain is cold. The old women trailing their skirts in the gutter screeching "Bootlaces!" or pushing handcarts haven't a thread on them that isn't soaked. The merchandise is soaked too—which is to say, ruined.

At the door of a public meeting, policemen provide a decoration. They think, under the driving rain, that it won't prevent freedom of speech this evening. Their brains, tightly bound by discipline, are haunted by revolutionary theories, which they have to remember as best they can for their reports.

In a house under construction, two children, a boy of about twelve, clad in a threadbare shirt and trousers, and a girl of nine or ten, have taken shelter. The little girl is entirely covered in rags; she has placed thereunder, in order to protect them, a few bouquets of violets and wallflowers, which she has been trying to sell since the morning.

The boy has a package on the end of a piece of string.

"Aren't you afraid of losing that?" says the little girl, pointing to the package. "It's not like my flowers. I'll lose six sous if they shed their petals."

"You might think that, little one. It's not sous that I'll lose if I let that rag fall apart because it's so badly tied up."

"What can it be? A cake? I found one of those myself, one morning when it was raining like today. A little dog had dropped it, while running away."

"You can't guess?"

"How do you expect me to guess, if it's not that? Anyway, if it were so precious, you wouldn't leave it dangling in the water."

"Idiot. If I'd carried it fondly in broad daylight, someone would have taken it off me."

"What can it be?"

Coming very close, he let fall the syllables: "Papers."

"Papers!" repeated the little girl, astonished. "Can you sell those?"

"No, little one; they're to be handed in to the law, to shed light on crimes about which there's a mystery."

"What can that dark lantern you're dangling on your piece of string shed light on?"

"The entire world, my girl. I've been offered a big reward—but I won't take it. I only want my conviction set aside."

Gertrude looked at André admiringly. In her eyes, he had grown as high as the clouds. André, stating his conditions to the magistrates, was refusing a reward that would permit him to eat as much as he wanted for a fortnight. André, with a conviction! He must at least have got mixed up in a strike!

With increasing dignity, he added: "You don't know why I've been convicted? It's because I escaped."

"Why were you in prison?"

"Because I have no parents, of course. Why would they have sent me to the penal colony otherwise?"

"To New Caledonia? You've already been to New Caledonia?"

"No, not that far, since I escaped by swimming. It was the daughter of a workman who got my collar off and gave me something to eat. I've been on the streets for a year; no one's recognized me yet; the girl promised me that she'd tell them that I'd drowned."

"You'll tell me all about it, won't you, André?"

"Yes, one day—when I have time."

"What do you have to do?"

"Well, go look for soup at the door of the mad-house, and then do my job. Père Lafortune lets me sleep on his rags in exchange for a basketful of worms every morning. He says that I serve as a guard-dog, to stop anyone stealing anything. He sells the worms to fisher-men."

"That's like me. Madame Tristan lets me sleep in a cupboard, in exchange for me picking up flowers that people throw away for her. I make them up into nice lit-tle bouquets; I have to bring back twenty sous every evening."

"What if you don't bring it back?"

"I go to bed without bread. But I was so hungry, you see, when I didn't bring back exactly twenty sous, that I ended up taking at least two sous in order to eat before going back, when I was short."

"And when you have more?"

"You think you're joking! We'll, I've had more. She only gets her franc, Madame Tristan! I give the rest to old Ursule, who likes me. You know old Ursule, who sells barley sugar. Once, she gave me one of them."

"Did you come into the world all alone?"

"No, I had a Mama. She threw us into the river one evening last winter, but a big dog pulled me out. I called to Mama, but I didn't throw myself back in—I was too cold and too frightened.

"I didn't go home; I started selling flowers that I picked up from the rubbish on my own. It was Madame Tristan who told me to stay with her, when she saw that I made nice new bouquets out of the old ones. 'That's the opposite of you,' a handsome gentleman said to Madame Tristan this morning. 'You make beautiful fresh flowers into dungheaps.' And they laughed so much, while looking at me, that I was scared. Nothing else scares me any longer, since Mama threw us in the water."

"You don't know why they laughed? I know—I'm older than you are. Madame Tristan wants to sell you."

"Sell me? That's what Mama said she didn't want anyone to do when she threw us in the water."

"You have to run away from that, Gertrude!"

"And where am I going to run to? I'll tell Madame Ursule. She'll help me."

"You don't know? Perhaps I can help you, since I'm going to do the law a favor."

The rain had stopped, and the two children, as sad as old people, emerged from their shelter. The sidewalk in front of them was all red; the water in the gutter was running pink.

An overladen horse that had slipped on the damp roadway had just collapsed there. Having lashed it with a thousand blows of the whip and having hit it with a stick, the coachman had noticed that it had a broken leg. One last kick, for the time it has cost him, provoked a terrible whinny. It was necessary to slaughter the beast on the spot; its leg was running like a spring, and they couldn't soil the sidewalk twice.

As the children drew apart they darted sad glances at the horse. Bah! There was no point shedding a tear for a dying animal while there were so many poor people still alive.

Isn't life worse than death?

VII. The House of the Lord

On the road from Colombes to Paris, there was, in the era of which we are speaking, a small house surrounded by high walls. Its roofs scarcely rose above them; one might have thought that it was a mausoleum.

Large tearful trees twist in the blast of the wind, which attacks them from all directions. Beggars, cripples, and sometimes travelers come there asking for help or shelter; it is the House of the Lord!

Three old women and a gardener live in the House of the Lord. During the night, the plaintive notes of some mysterious song can be heard coming from it, but never anything during the day.

The three women rarely go out and receive no visits except those of an old man with pinched lips and a broad forehead with green-tinted eyes, who might have resembled Nostradamus or Mesmer if he didn't bear a closer resemblance to Shylock. No one in the neighborhood knows the old man's name; in the House of the Lord he is known as the High Priest, the Djaina Chala Sarma.[12]

This High Priest has, like the old ones, lived several lives; he claims to be able to remember them; the women don't doubt him.

All possible and impossible conjectures have been exhausted with regard o the House of the Lord; its leg-

---

[12] I have retained a slightly-Anglicized version of the original text's Djaïna rather than translating it into the more familiar Jain, because it is quite obvious that "Chala Sarma" is not a Jain at all.

end has been formed, as legends are, with a little truth beneath the darkness.

That grain of truth is that the three women met, as beings tormented by the same idea do meet, after having carried out more-or-less serious experiments together, to which their wonderstruck minds gave confidence; they came together, driven by the thirst for the supernatural, which they sought. It was not the devouring ardor of science, however, which reasons, hollows out, breaks or saves human lives; it was an impassioned love of the marvelous: the marvelous that lulls life, like the nursery tales that charm childhood.

In order to shiver together at the slightest sound, to feel fear passing over them, without taking account of it, in savoring that enjoyment—fear experienced in total security—first two of them, and then three, had come together.

Like the Norns, or the Parcae,[13] and also a little like the Furies, the three old women attempted, with heartfelt sincerity, the mysterious or insensate rites that the High Priest indicated to them.

One of these three fantastic creatures had ended up obtaining, by chance, what she wanted: strange things. She had an immense empire over the other two; veritable magnetic effluvia were emitted by her person. The same thing happens in lunatic asylums. Karpa had acquired some of the abilities of fakirs. The other two, Holda and Nara, nearer to the ordinary, were the reflection of the first—her moons, the High Priest Chala Sarma called them. The house, usually sepulchrally quiet, was filled at time with an immense life; torches were lit; songs rose into the air with perfumes.

---

[13] i.e., the Fates.

That was because the Djaina was presiding over a sacrifice.

A pyre of odorous wood orientated to the four winds, in order that the victims ashes would be carried thereto, was lit in a vulgar stove. While the Djaina explained that, in one of his former lives, he had been placed on a pyre before Alexander on the banks of the Indus, demonstrating to the conqueror that Djainas could triumph over pain, and the victim, a black chicken or a pigeon, solidly secured by the feet in place of the raised lid, beat its wings in the flames, the three women sang in chorus the words of the sanyasis[14] rendered into bad French verse:

> Prepare the robe of flame,
> The svarga[15] requires a pyre.
> To the four winds Brahma's choir
> With the ashes will climb.

For a long time, there had been nothing on the stove's perfumed pyre but pigeons or black chickens, fanning the flames with their crazed wings.

One night in autumn, the Jain replied to the chorus of the women in a terrible voice:

> The svarga's desires an abundance
> Of blood spilled on the pyre;
> Else a war will break out
> In which the world will collapse.

---

[14] Sannyasa is the way of life of a Hindu "renouncer" or ascetic.

[15] The author adds a footnote defining *svarga* as "corpse."

Karpa shivered; the other two huddled against her, moaning, while the Djaina, lighting a torch from the pyre, waved it in the air as if to reply to the svarga.

For seven days and seven nights they fasted and prayed; then the Djaina returned and told them that the svarga demanded the sacrifice of Pékian; the goat-kid that followed Karpa was tied upon the pyre, its head and breast protruding in order that it my scream for longer at the deaf heavens.

Impassively, the three hypnotized women contemplated the beast, turning its eyes toward its mistress in the torments that twisted it like a green vine-branch.

Another seven days passed, seven being a fateful number, in fasting and prayers. The svarga remained mute; there was a great sadness in the House of the Lord; the poor received their daily pittance without going inside, the bread was renewed, and even the gardener did not cross the threshold of the third room—"the parvis of the temple," as it was called in the House of the Lord. The names of his mistresses were unknown to him, for the mysterious appellations Karpa (the acme of celestial felicity), Holda (the Celtic Sabbath) and Nara (the Indian virgin, spouse of Nari)[16] did not cross the sacred threshold; Thomas the gardener simply called them Madame la Grande, Madame la Jeune and Madame la Petite—and, profane as he was, he said privately:

---

[16] None of these supposed meanings seems to be correct, nor can I find any probable misspellings that would yield those definitions (the second name is rendered Halda the first time it appears and Harpa here, but I have generalized a later rendering that seems more suitable, by virtue of its use in Germanic folklore in association with witchcraft, and hence with a Sabbath of sorts.)

Madame la Sèche, Madame la Toquée and Madame Béquillarde.[17]

As for the Djaina, as no one but him ever entered into the intimacy of the three Parcae, Thomas referred to him prosaically as "Monsieur," making him a pendant of the stove that served as a pyre.

The house belonged to the youngest of the three, who had taken in the other two. All three were miserly, fearful of being in need in their old age—which would have deprived them of the soothing effects of the mystic life, something more frightening to them than the loss of life.

There was someone even more miserly than them; that was the Djaina Chala Sarma, whose real name was Eleazer. He was a dealer in curiosities, trafficking in works of art, loans at two hundred per cent interest and various other business arrangements, whose wife ran a matrimonial agency, procuring, placing and displacing fresh flesh, and branches of a similar order—or, rather, tentacles of the same octopus.

---

[17] The author adds a parenthetical note defining *béquillarde* as "lame" (or, "on crutches"); *sèche*, in this context, means "stiff" or "withered," *toquée* "crack-brained" or "daft."

VIII. Inconvenient Details

Being convinced that instinct alone could cry out against him, but knowing that humans no longer make use of that alarm system, Roll, fully exposed to the dangers of his situation, was still only thinking of warding them off as they cropped up.

Bah! he said to himself. *It's a matter of a few days.*

A life of identical studies had sufficiently imprinted both twins with the particular stamp of scholars for their mannerisms, already similar, to become even more so.

He allowed himself to be guided by Anna, following the indications that the anticipations of the poor woman revealed to him.

In the dining-room, he rediscovered his own tastes: the grotesque, the eccentric and the horrible. The paintings there represented the legendary meals of ghouls in the depths of cemeteries; scenes of murder; monstrous feasts in which drunken males and females were inflated and deflated like balloons; scenes of the legendary Sabbat and the Sabbat of life. Yes, he really was his brother! Perhaps, now that the other was dead, Roll's life was doubled.

At that thought, he thought he heard a howl of laughter in his ear.

Could such an impression give him pause? He shook himself and started laughing freely and gaily, as if he had never left the house where he was. Suddenly, he stopped. Anna was staring at him with an indefinable expression; it was instinct returning.

"What's the matter with me?" he said.

"I don't know! Something strange. I'm worried."

Roll smiled and replied: "I've been reading some hallucination by Edgar Poe; it raises a fog around you."

For a second time, he heard the same small sound, plaint or laughter, that had struck him before.

At the same time, Étienne opened the door, and a little black dog hurtled into the rom.

"Monsieur forgot Diane yesterday," said Étienne. "Fortunately, I went into the garden; she was locked in the shed."

He had not finished speaking when Diane, her fur bristling, had placed herself in front of Roll, sniffing his clothes, and leapt at his throat.

With hands like pincers he seized her by the neck and threw her to the floor, dead.

"She was rabid," he said, coldly.

Once the anxiety for Roll had passed, Anna and the old man spared a regret for poor Diane; she had belonged to Anna's mother. It was inexplicable; she had caressed Étienne a few minutes before, when he had found her locked in the shed.

"She was already sick when I locked her up," Roll said. "I forgot her."

It seemed to Anna that her husband had a trickle of blood on his wrist; she wanted to roll up the sleeve—it was the arm marked with the Hebrew *reich*. Roll resisted. It was nothing... it was ridiculous.

The rest of the morning was mournful.

When Roll was able to retire to his study, he rolled up the sleeve and saw where the drop of blood had come from. There was a large bead of it on a puncture similar to than made by an awl—the imprint of one of Diane's teeth.

Courageously, he placed the blade of a pen-knife reddened in a candle-flame upon it; he could not ask for anything without risking the *reich* being seen.

The animal was not rabid, but in its anger it was dangerous. Moreover, the tooth had not passed through his clothing, but the flesh; he did not understand how.

Bah! Could rabies afflict him? Scornful laughter took hold of him again.

The most difficult part is over, he thought, acquiring more ample cognizance of the projects and papers of every sort in the judge's filing-cabinet. *The landing has been made.*

Indeed, the landing had been made, but would Anna's love for Philippe always be deceived? Anna had animated her husband's marble heart; she was experiencing an anxiety for which she could not account. That was because the current of love that existed between them had been cut off, since Philippe was dead.

Roll's presence had filled the house with anguish; the kind of atmosphere reigned there that makes dogs howl at death. It was necessary to force the children to go to their father; Étienne noticed things that nearly drove the poor old fellow made with anxiety. The house became stranger and more somber by the day.

After a few days, matters took on an even greater monstrousness. The passion that had awakened in Roll enveloped Anna, enlacing her and burning her like a garment of flame.

Some amours are rabid; it was thus between the murderer and his victim's widow.

Anna had never loved her husband with that savage passion. The broad space opened in her heart by the children had never experienced such wrenching heartache, and had never been so small.

IX. Various Captures

As events transpired, it was Roll who was, thanks to Philippe's reputation, entrusted with the investigation of his own crime.

The mystery of the Railway Bridge was still complicated; it was not the murderers who were unknown but their victim. The gold stolen by the murderers, the inspection of the hands utterly unused to hard labor and the care taken to render the victim unrecognizable all proved that the unknown man was rich. A search was mounted for important individuals who had disappeared; there were none, foreigners or otherwise.

He must have been some political refugee, obliged to hide.

Roll, smitten by a sudden compassion for outcasts, had enquiries made with the goal of arriving at a real identity, on which he would build his drama. There was only one political individual of whom no trace could be found. He was the treasurer of a Philanthropic Society who had fled with its funds. That did not suit Roll's purpose. In any case, the Chairman of the Society in question, who knew that a few minor papers of his own were in the hands of the runaway, was able to prove that he was not dead. That trail was abandoned.

The victim remained unidentified, but Roll, not giving up on the idea of a political refugee, took note of the fact that Jacques had been seen at popular meetings. How could the crime committed by the sculptor be explained otherwise? He had evidently been given orders by someone else—that was, moreover, what Pierre had

47

confessed. A man had promised him a large sum; his child was dying of poverty; he had obeyed.

As for recognizing that man in the person of Jacques, Pierre would not do it—but do not criminals make such provisions for their accomplices?

One day, driven to an extreme by the examining magistrate, Pierre looked at him audaciously, pointing at Jacques, and replied: "With all due respect, Monsieur le Juge, the man who instructed me to commit the crime bore a closer resemblance to you than to him."

Pierre had insulted a judge in the exercise of his duty, and was returned to his cell severely. The investigation followed its course without him being called again. It mattered little to him, as we know.

Jacques did not remember anything himself, from the moment that an unknown man, of whom he had only seen the eyes, had filled his hands with gold. At first he had thought about flinging it in his face, but then a terrible thirst had gripped him. He had gone into the café, asked for something to drink, and had woken up in prison. They could interrogate him for as long as he lived. Roll coldly pinned him down with impossibilities; it was a yarn he was spinning, which did not stand up.

Marthe, concentrated in her pain, no longer made any reply. Why bother?

The investigation reached its end.

The newspapers saw a gang of murderers, some of whom had been arrested.

On the first day of the Assizes, the hall was too small to contain those thirsty for emotion, curiosity-seekers and a few physiologists—who, searching the features, accents and gaits of the accused, found traces of criminality.

An autograph letter by Jacques was sold for a hundred francs and a charcoal sketch for a thousand, to a old gentleman who found infallible indications of crime therein.

Another proposed that it was the same with all those whose affinities attracted them to public meetings. The miasmas of murder, pillage and arson, etc., etc., were disengaged therefrom.

A lady with pupils steeped in mysticism, dreamed about of accusing herself, in all their details, to Abbé Cadet,[18] her spiritual advisor, of the horrible things to which she had exposed herself to seeing and hearing.

The reading of the indictment put an end to all other preoccupations.

The crime was proven; Pierre had confessed. If he was obstinate in refusing to recognize his accomplice, it was because his terror had not passed; the blow had been struck on behalf of a political party; the Internationale was involved; the very silence of the groups proved their complicity. Their prudence, however, had been betrayed by a friend of Jacques, an accomplice, who had tried to send him, in prison, a cutting from a newspaper containing an account of his crime, hidden in a large nutshell.

That wasn't very smart, but there was more than the nutshell, and simpler. The friend had asked to testify.

---

[18] This character cannot possibly be Pierre de St. Stevin Abbé, who was known as Abbé Cadet in order to distinguish him from his elder brother, with whom he had performed as a cellist at the Grand Opéra long before the time of the story, and seems to have passed himself off as a priest, but the borrowing of the name is suggestive of an imposture, or at least of hypocrisy.

Testify to what? That was a guarantee of grave responsibility.

The charge-sheet, like the speech for the prosecution, called for the utmost severity of the law. As for the victim, so artfully disfigured, the world would learn one day, with terror, which illustrious individual was missing at roll-call!

No one could have accumulated plausible circumstances better than Roll. The mystery that covered the victim cast a vague terror over the affair. Everyone who thought he was important imagined death suspended overhead.

The testimony of the witnesses revealed nothing new.

The tavern-keeper of the Clichy road, the owner of the café in which Jacques had been arrested and all the people who were there testified to what they had seen. The Haut-Marnais, having proved that he knew nothing, was excused from making the journey; Rose had dearly wanted to see an Assize Court, but, whether she liked it or not, she declared, like her father, that they had left before any incident had occurred.

As the old joker who had been with the young whore in the café, having dragged her away very rapidly, did not want his wife to know who he had been dallying with so late at night, the witness evidence offered no interest, and the interrogation was limited to one of the accused confessing his guilt in a grim fashion and the other denying it in a even more brutal fashion. Marthe had not wanted to reply.

One incident changed the face of things: a boy of about twelve, thin and small for his age, persistently demanded to be heard; he said that he had papers to hand over to the law. "It's the identity of the victim," he pro-claimed, in an emphatic voice.

The order having been given to throw him out, he had to be heard because of the public outcry.

The papers were contained in an elegant wallet, which was disengaged from the greasy envelope in which André had been carrying them around for more than three months on the end of a piece of string.

Motionless at the door, little Gertrude was waiting anxiously for André to come out.

"What is this wallet?" the president demanded of André, who was being eyed by two gendarmes.

"I picked it up under the arches where the man was found." As he spoke he handed it to an usher, who presented it to the judge.

The wallet, a dainty receptacle of Russian leather, the color of earth, would easily have escaped the initial investigations. Placing it on the table in front of him, the president proceeded with a summary interrogation of the witness.

"What is your name?"

"André."

"Where were you born?"

"I don't know."

"How old are you?"

"Twelve, I think."

"Where do you live?"

"Monsieur Lafortune lodges me in exchange for a basket of worms every morning."

"Where does he live?"

"The Rag-Pickers' city in Montmartre."

"Why hasn't he come with you?"

"No one knows what I found."

"Because you've kept quiet?"

"Yes, Monsieur le Juge—I was afraid someone would nick it."

"Do you want to be rewarded?"

"Oh, no, not at all, Monsieur le Juge. All I've ever wanted is…for my condemnation to be revoked."

"Your condemnation?"

"Yes. I ran away from where I was."

"Where were you? And why did you run away?"

"I was in La Chylokière."[19]

"A penitentiary colony! Arrest this wretch—he's in breach of a restriction order."

This was done immediately. André was obliged to sit down between the two gendarmes who kept an eye on him—but his confidence in the law was unshaken.

In spite of his audacity, Roll had sensed a little shiver pass through his flesh.

The first paper was a letter:

Monsieur,

The hypnotism session will take place, as usual, in my drawing-room in the Avenue de Clichy, on Friday afternoon. I do not think it necessary for you to take the precaution of coming on foot from the Place de Wagram. No one here or in the vicinity knows you. There will be, in addition to the usual program, general studies of the

---

[19] The name of this fictitious establishment is sometimes rendered "Chilokérie," but that does not make its possible etymology any easier to interpret. There is no reason why a Frenchification of "Shylockery" should be used in this context, and if the word is derived from the English it is more likely that it comes from "child lockery" or perhaps "child rookery" (the author and many of her readers would have been familiar with the contemporary application of the term "rookery" to a slum inhabited by criminals).

magnetic fluid, made by an extra-lucid somnambulist,
Madame Lucrèce.
Accept, Monsieur le Magistrat, my urgent regards.

DR. MARTIALI
28 May 18**

Roll realized that he was in trouble. The wallet must be his brother's, and the papers it contained might involve surprises for him. His hairy body was infested with a cold sweat. His face expressed no emotion, however—not enough, for the other judges were rendered anxious by a keen curiosity. The president had passed on the letter, which lacked an envelope.

Monsieur le juge! The victim was a magistrate then?

Roll waited for the discoveries to conclude, in order to respond to everything, without one reckoning being able to demolish the other.

A second piece of paper was in the judge's hands, again lacking an envelope. Philippe had definitely been prudent, but that devil of a Dr. Martiali must be known in the Avenue de Clichy; he would be questioned. So what? Could not Roll display Philippe, alive, before everyone?

Paris, 15 May 18**
Monsieur le juge,
I am imploring you to defend my daughter and myself we are guilty but I wanted and still only want to save her; let everything fall on me, that's what I mean by defending me.

Reine Félix
4 Rue de Belleville

This Reine Félix must know to which advocate or magistrate she had addressed that plea. Her letter passed, like the others, through the hands of all the judges.

The silence was so profound that the labored breath of two individuals who had just come in, with some difficulty, could be heard. They were huddling in a corner, not taking up much space, and taking a passionate interest in the affair. The eyes of strange couple, one a man, fully dressed this time, and the other a woman whose dress still bore the particular label of the shop where she had bought it for the occasion, were drinking in the tribunal, the accused, the gendarmes, and sometimes surveying the audience a glance similar to that of an actor coming on stage, sure of being in character.

The effect that they were going to produce, they thought, would efface the effect produced by the wallet.

Scientific notes—unsigned—occupied several sheets. Why the devil had Philippe interested himself in such things? Roll had been misinformed; it was not to see a mistress that his brother was going to the Avenue de Clichy, but to attend a scientific meeting.

The mistress might have killed herself—but would that devil-cat Reine talk?

He began, therefore, whisper to the others that the wallet had been stolen, that the child was a young blackmailer, who should be returned very rapidly to the penal colony of La Chylokière.

These things were circulated, like the papers, in whispers, in such a fashion that the members of the jury, in whose hands the two letters now were, were made aware of them.

The president was holding a third piece of paper, in which there was a lock of blonde hair—doubtless the object that had been put in the hands of the somnambulist. Roll recognized Anna's blonde hair. Philippe had not had another lover! It was a childish letter in large handwriting. That would not reveal anything; he had nothing to fear in that direction. Philippe had doubtless had the idea of sending the somnambulist to the establishment mentioned by the boy. A less vaporous search would have been more valuable, Roll thought. This time he was right.

Mossieu, the letter said, *wen you cam today to strik a bargin, I cud not say that Pierre is [halaquerapodinne] and olso ther's summing else, I deman justis mossieu your life is at stak. Jacot.* (No date or address.)[20]

"Jacot! He came in the day I escaped!" exclaimed André, between the two gendarmes.

The wallet had definitely been stolen, André must have slipped that letter from his comrade into it before bringing it; there was nothing to be done but send the fellow back to La Chylokière, with some stern notes in red ink. The incident had nothing to do with the crime; but information must be obtained with due diligence—that was the magistrates' opinion.

---

[20] I have reproduced the "word" in square brackets directly from the original, being unable to venture a possible translation. When this passage was written there was presumably an intention that this mangled text would reveal something about Roll's initial approach to Pierre to some subsequent enquirer, but no further reference is made to the letter or its writer, and it remains one of the more mysterious of the plot's many loose ends.

"And what about this? Is this stolen too? It was in the victim's hands—they didn't undress his hands!" cried the shrill voice of La Greluchette and the gurgling voice of Jean Hénoe.

This time Roll felt himself go pale. His brother must have worn rings! Bah! It was another theft.

A new emotion stirred the crowd. It was necessary, in spite of the singularity of their appearance, to let the people speak. They could, they said, establish the identity of the victim.

If the man had had solid shoes and his trousers had had two similar legs, he would have been able to find his footing, and his deposition would have been less firm, but since the night before, having nothing more to sell, and no work, he had drunk nothing but water from the fountains. He earned his bread every morning by sweeping the floor of a bakery; that was where he lived.

La Greluchette lived with him—forever they said—nibbling the same bread, to which she sometimes added, as she put it, a sweetener. She had bought for the assizes, from a clothing shop, a second-hand dress for herself and headgear—a cap—for Jean Hénoe.

There they were, the two of them, between the spectacles of the magistrates and the monocles, opera-glasses and nose-pinchers of the audience. Gazes searched beneath their rags, all the way to the bones. There they were, poor wretches, holding in their hands the key to a mystery, one of the most exciting.

"Sit down, witnesses."

Pointing to Jean Hénoe: "Come forward."

"Your name?"

"Jean Hénoe."

"Your age?"

"Well, I don't know, exactly. When Père Hénoe told me he wasn't my father, he forgot to tell me how he'd found me, or the number of my years."

"You don't know your civil status?"

"I don't even know what civil is. As for my status, I've turned my hand to all sorts. Is it my fault if I don't have a status? I work hard when I can, though!"

"Be brief!"

"You're the one that asked me. It's not about that. Here's the gloves! Eh? They're facts! You won't find others like that, with such a palm! A real wolf's paw!"

Indeed, the palm was unusually broad. That had been observed with respect to the cadaver's soft white hand. That was why there was doubt rather than denial on the part of the tribunal.

"Where did you find those gloves?"

"We heard the fight, La Greluchette and me; we were passing…"

"Why didn't you go for help for the victim?"

"I wasn't steady on my feet and La Greluchette isn't strong."

"Who is this Greluchette?"

"It's Madame, who has come to give evidence with me."

"Recount the facts."

"Well, Madame and I had just taken a walk. It was dark, we were singing on the road to the fortifications. I can even remember the song:

> The juice of the vine
> Makes the face red
> In drunkenness!"

Roll remembered.

The man continued: "La Greluchette can back me up—it was the third verse I was singing, when there was something..."

"Be brief, witness."

"Well then, we heard I big *oof*, as if someone had bashed someone, but we said, it's nothing; things like that happen at night, and one never knows what will come of it. There are folk who kill one another; that's their right—me, I'd rather drink."

"The facts."

"We went nearer. The man had been fighting with two others, and one said crush his face, undress him. We couldn't save him without waiting for the murderers to go. I was sobering up, but I couldn't stand up.

"After the victim was alone, we went over, but there was nothing to be done. The throat was cut almost right through—no means to bring him back to life. Then I said to La Greluchette: we must avenge him."

"What did she say?"

"I'd felt the gloves and the rings underneath; they'd enough to identify him, I said. Then we took off the gloves and pulled off the rings. There are the gloves. La Greluchette will let you see the rings."

While Jean Hénoe was telling the story the gloves were passing, as the papers had, from hand to hand, from the judges to the jury.

A Corsican affair, thought one.

The mystery's unraveling, thought the others.

That'll bring the criminals down a peg, thought La Greluchette.

In the meantime, Roll gazed gravely at the gloves with the wide palms. The judge sitting next to him, having darted a glance at Roll's hands, blushed to the ears when he noticed that the gloves would have fit his colleague marvelously. (That was a crime of *lèse-justice*.)

Roll sensed the glance and collected himself, in order to get himself out of the tight spot.

It was La Greluchette's turn.

The general opinion was that these witnesses would have some difficulty getting out of the terrible hands of the law.

"What is your name?"

"Claire Germain, known as La Greluchette."

"How old are you?"

"Twenty."

"Where were you born?"

"In Quimper."

"Why did you come to Paris?"

"To go into service. My parents were dead."

"The same old story. Do you have a place?"

"I haven't had one for a year. A beautiful lady took me away."

"What is your status?"

"Domestic, of course."

"And now?"

La Greluchette did not reply.

"Where do you live?"

"With Jean Hénoe."

"In furnished lodgings?"

"When we can."

"Why haven't you sought another position?"

"I couldn't. They asked for my papers, and Madame hadn't wanted me to be reported to a monsieur who was following me everywhere and others who came to her house."

"Be brief! Where are the rings the witness alleged to be in your possession."

"Here!" La Greluchette gave the usher a cardboard box tied up with string.

Emptied on to the table, the box let three rings escape, of such value that the judges started.

The drama was not over.

The president stood up and, addressing La Greluchette and Jean Hénoe, and demanded that Jacques repeat before them the words "Crush the face," which they had heard.

Jacques stood up, repeated the words in a terrible tone, and, combining that with a terrible action, launched himself toward the evidence table, which was placed below that of the judges, and on which was set the blood-stained stone that had served to crush the victim's face. With a robust arm whose strength was doubled by anger, Jacques lifted the enormous weight of the stone and, bracing himself on his legs, hurled the stone at the president's face. It almost reached him, and caused ink from the overturned inkwells to splash the judges' faces.

Jacques was thrown out of the courtroom and did not appear there again, in spite of the protests of the lawyer who had been appointed to defend him in spite of his wishes.

After his departure the president continued: "These rings, like the wallet, could have come from some other victim. The law will investigate. I propose to the tribunal a postponement until the next session."

It was a matter of keeping the three witnesses in prison until further notice.

Jean Hénoe cried: "We haven't told everything—there's another pair of gloves: those of the murderer. That's funny, for sure! All the funnier because one would think they'd been made for the same hands!"

That was the reflection the judges made as they passed on to the second pair of gloves.

"It's quite simple," Roll whispered. "There are people who put on a fresh pair of gloves when they go into a drawing-room. Both pairs must belong to the victim."

That affirmation was imprudent on Roll's part; things were becoming threatening! But between now and the following week he had time in hand. The investigation would only be carried out by him. Then again, he knew that the court, having all the elements, proposed to hold another hearing.

The affair, as reported by the newspapers, took on immense proportions the following day. They had decided that there must be a redoubtable association, of which little André, Jean Hénoe and La Greluchette were merely docile instruments.

The drama embraced an immense horizon.

X. *The Hebrew* Reich

Who can say how thoughtful Anna became on reading newspaper reports of the trial?

The rings, of which the reporters had given a detailed description, were preoccupying her thoughts.

At lunch, she inspected Roll's hands: those hands with the broad palms, similar to those of the victim! There were resemblances, but it was the first time she had found so many strange circumstances in combination.

The jewels, similar to those she had been accustomed to seeing on Philippe's fingers, twisted in her heart like a wound.

Étienne, for his part, found the atmosphere of the house heavy. He sought to distract himself by buying the newspapers that were being hawked everywhere. The poor old dog, his head heavy and his heart full of anguish, scented a trail, finding it everywhere and nowhere. His thoughts roamed the shadows; he shut himself away in his room.

Was it not crazy to keep reading eternally about that affair, which had nothing to do with anything? For a long time, Étienne had not seen the rings on his master's fingers—for they were the three rings that Philippe had worn since his marriage: the ring exchanged with Anna and two diamond rings that had been handed down to her from her family.

Étienne was haunted by a singular image: Diane, her fur bristling, her eyes ardent, prowling around him.

The children, at present, were fearful every night; the wind was blowing in the Red Room; they no longer wanted to sleep there.

"You won't be scared any more, my dears," Anna said. "I'll stay with you."

Indeed, when evening came, she sang them to sleep. The voice froze on her cold lips; it seemed to her that the wind was sad—and yet the children went to sleep.

It was not that Roll had any remorse; he had not the slightest scruple—no, it was passion that enveloped him, putting fire in his veins, throwing him on to an unknown path.

Can a man who has gone into a field where the scythed grass is drying on the ground escape the bitter odor spread through the air?

Pursued by the life that he had made for himself, Roll moved through the fiery atmosphere of his brother's house.

Under the tropical sun his brain had made broad thrusts, but his breast had remained mute. Now his heart was awakening.

Like those who throw themselves into the water with a stone tied around their neck, Roll felt himself sliding into the black depths of destiny. He felt a cold current pass over his heart, and sought to regain his self-possession.

That evening, however, his strength had diminished; he knew that Anna, inattentive until now with regard the disappearance of the rings, would have read the newspapers, that she would look at his hands.

Certainly, he would have no difficulty finding reasons, but he was apprehensive.

For the first time, Roll felt his heart bleed, and he burst into sobs. Then getting a grip on himself again, with impassioned force, he went to see Anna in the room where the children were sleeping.

"Anna," he said, "professional secrecy, even with respect to those one loves, is an obligation greater than life itself."

She raised her head, which was leaning on the bed where her children were asleep. They awoke crying. It was the wind again, they said! The mother's instinct awoke; she wanted to stay with them—but he summoned Étienne, put the weeping infants into the old man's arms, and took the mother away.

As he consoled them, the old man thought about poor Diane, whose image haunted him in spite of himself.

Roll recaptured Anna's love.

In the morning, having gone to sleep with one of his arms on the coverlet, Roll had left that arm uncovered, the sleeve bunched up, exposing, marked as in the days of his childhood, the Hebrew *reich* that, as Philippe had told his wife a hundred times, distinguished them from one another.

The horrible story appeared to her. She got up calmly, understanding everything.

The murdered man was Philippe; she knew the secret of his visits to the home of Dr. Martiali, the letters, the rings; completing all that, the Hebrew letter put the seal on the discovery.

Anna went to the children's room, silently. In that house of death she moved like a shadow.

Étienne, leaning on the bed had gone to sleep late, his arm still passed over the children, as if to guard them even in their sleep.

Anna woke him up, and spoke abruptly. "Père Étienne! Come on! We're leaving! I don't know where. I'll tell you. Come on! Don't waste any time!"

Hastily, they took a few clothes and some money, and, no one else having got up as yet, took the children away without attracting any attention.

When he awoke, Roll looked down at his exposed arm, and felt a chill in the marrow of his bones.

Anna, the old man and the children had disappeared.

Roll's despair was terrible.

Anna knew everything! Everything! And he loved her madly, now; he loved the children as though they were his own—and everything was crumbling.

It had to be a dream, a nightmare.

He walked back and forth for a few moments, breathing deeply, his teeth clenched, revealing their enamel beneath his thin lips.

His savage nature was reclaiming its rights.

The day had dawned bright and joyful; the deserted rooms were full of its light; Roll heard the domestics getting up.

The latter rarely saw the masters; there was nothing to fear on that front. But Anna! Old Étienne!

So what? Who could attack him? Would not anyone who did be considered mad by everyone else?

Madame and the children had gone to the country. Roll shut himself up in his study. His love for Anna was doubled by an immense hatred against humankind entire. He did not even know whether what he was experiencing for her was pain or love.

XI. The Judgment of the Tribunal

Roll was brilliant, great and magnanimous when he stood up, in the interests of justice, voluntarily surrendering his prestige, saying: "I need to enlighten Messieurs the judges and Messieurs the jurors regarding the various incidents of the last session."

It was beyond doubt, not only that they were dealing with a redoubtable political association, to which no crime was too costly in order to attain its ends, but that the ramifications extended so far that the jewels, stolen from the examining magistrate himself in order to be sold to the profit of some dark endeavor, were to have served to lead justice astray instead. At any rate, he would tell the truth, no matter what it cost him.

An old man, who had seen him born, in whom he had had boundless confidence, had now fled, after having delivered his master's jewels to the organization of which a few affiliates were in custody, and, with the aim of misleading the Court, a vile comedy had been played at the previous hearing.

Roll's story, told in a dramatic fashion, excited the audience profoundly.

The entire tribunal bowed down before him when, having confessed his scientific curiosities—a tribute that he paid to his century—he dragged out the name of the wretch who had stolen from him.

He had scarcely been able to pronounce, slowly, with profound regret, the syllables of the name *Étienne*, henceforth consigned to infamy, when an old man emerged from one of the corners of the hall, where he had been waiting to dissipate the final doubts.

Forcing his way through, so much strength did he find in his indignation, he arrived at the foot of the tribunal. "That's a lie!" he cried, in a terrible voice. "I, Étienne, say that it's a lie!"

Roll went pale, but he had no need to worry; the old man collapsed like an inert mass, the blood having flowed away from his heart.

The tragic impression of that death caused the hearing to be adjourned until the following day.

A few papers were found in poor Étienne's pockets. One of these papers was a receipt for the lease of a small detached house, paid in advance, by Madame d'Erfel. D'Erfel was Anna's maiden name.

Roll now knew where to find her.

The house was in Argenteuil. Patiently, he waited for nightfall.

The night was a little warmer than the night of the crime; it was August, and the earth, warmed all day by the sun, exhaled the effluvia of the day into the darkness.

Overwhelmed by the terrible struggle that the dangers of his situation and the fever of his crime had put to sleep, Roll walked along the road from Paris to Argenteuil toward the house rented by Madame d'Erfel. Now the frightful ideality of the situation loomed up before the monster, as if, half-transformed, the human part would have liked to tear itself bloodily away from its bestial envelope, or retreat back into it entirely, surrendering to its passion, which the difficulties were causing to increase without limits. On one side was the Seine, on the other, the solitary boulevard that leads to the railway station, lined with tall trees.

Roll got his bearings automatically, scenting the nest where Anna was hiding with the children.

There was no concierge. The isolated house was surrounded by hedges, which Roll got through easily.

A lamp was lit in the second room. Anna was sitting in there with the children.

Étienne could not be on the threshold. With his broad-palmed hands, as muscular as the limbs of a wild beast, Roll broke a ground-floor window and, like the limp rag he was, fell at Anna's feet, bloodied by the fragments of the panes and racked by sobs.

She ran to her sons' cot.

"Listen—I can explain!"

"Back, murderer! Don't deny it!"

"Well, yes, I'm a murderer—but I love you! I'm horrified by myself, by the entire world! My life is in your hands."

He struck the floor with his forehead, repeating: "Anna! Anna!"

She made no reply, leaving him there, like an earthworm, in the annihilation of his entire being and the confession of his crime.

Vengeance, hared for the wife and horror, rising in his heart, disputed there with the monstrous passion that had enveloped him, and still enveloped him.

The children, waking up, called to their mother, under the empire of the strange terror of the wind that had gripped them in the Red Room.

In the face of Roll's frightening dolor, Anna sensed her hatred vanquished, horrible love gripping her again, tearing at her heart. With the children clinging to her neck, mute with terror, she launched herself through the broken window into the profound darkness, toward the Seine.

Roll followed the fugitive trace of her dress in the darkness. He did not catch up with her, and, while close behind her, he heard a dull sound. The livid water formed broad circles.

In vain he dived in, fighting the current; in vain he exerted himself to search the green-tinted shroud; Anna and the children had been carried away by the current.

Roll was in despair; the magnitude of the struggle, in which he seemed to have the entire world and a part of himself against him, gave him strength. He did not want to be beaten, and, exerting all his will-power to dominate himself, he appeared at the resumption of the hearing, and formulated precise details with a marvelous logic. The accused were doomed.

Jacques and Pierre were condemned to death, Marthe, Jean Hénoe and La Greluchette to life imprisonment with hard labor.

André was sent back to La Chylokière, with notes in red ink.

Gertrude waited at the door of the Palais de Justice for a long time, thinking that he would come out laden with honors, but when night fell she was obliged to go back to Madame Tristan, without a sou—and in spite of the lies that fear forced her to find, Gertrude went to bed without bread, after having received a generous distribution of hammer-blows.

It was the correction she dreaded; Gertrude was too sad to be hungry.

Perhaps André, covered with honors and rewards that he could not refuse, had forgotten her! Rolling that thought around her empty head, the child ended up going to sleep, slumber scarcely drying up her tears.

Roll, having returned to the empty house, felt on his raw wound the irritation of the delicacy the magistrates had brought to talking about the theft in which he was concerned—that circumspection exercised in his regard felt like needles being stuck into his living flesh.

A few weeks after the judgment, the two death sentences were commuted, the executioner having been so maladroit during the previous execution as to have evoked horror.

XII. The Red Cock

In convict prisons, the inmates go to bed early. Why stay up? The limbs can do no more; nothing more can be got out of them. What point is there in giving the brain time to be awake? One has no need of thinking to work standing up; only muscular force is employed.

The brains devote themselves nevertheless to elaborating the ideas that choke them. Couched on hard bunks, the convicts relate strange things, sometimes so fresh that one feels purified beneath their wings, usually so somber that they frighten those who do not know the true state of things.

The responsibility of the old stepmother of civilized society—who throws three quarters of her children into the stream and fishes them out in order to surround them with all miseries, while the fourth quarter is destined for the corruption of wealth—would be enormous, if society itself were completely responsible on our raft of the *Medusa*.

In the convict prison there are the abandoned; there are the impassioned drawn out like wire by life, like horses trained to race; there are the innocent; there are noble characters fallen together into exile by what is called humanity; there are a few destinies bogged down by vanity; and there are also monsters, as there are everywhere.

If one looks at a lunatic asylum, the same cases present themselves: the mania of power; the mania of love; the mania of wealth; the mania of despair. Bells round the neck and crimes have the same causes.

It is a cold night in winter; the window-panes are covered in arabesques of frost; a bitter wind is blowing from the sea, also bitter on the earth. The room is icy; perhaps, in an hour or two, the breath of those heaped up there will create warm currents.

There has been a revolt during the day; it has been stifled, but fire is brooding beneath the ashes; there's too much suffering! Why care about one's life? If the opportunity has been missed, another will come along, however small it might be.

At first, there is an interval of stupid fear, the flock awaiting the next day's punishment. One man, however, raises his head in the midst of the general stupor, and the others look at him fearfully. Some signal to him to lie down again; it's forbidden to raise one's head! Tomorrow's punishment will be doubled for the unruly sheep.

The man's ardent eyes stare into space; he shrugs his shoulders, looking around in the wan gleam of the night-lights. He studies the lugubrious scene intently; he could reproduce it if he were an artist.

That gaze, which is not addressed to anyone, emits a warmth, and reignites the revolt. Searching the hairless faces in the morbid light, the man recalls them to life.

The scene of this living morgue can only be rendered by a sketch or a painter seeking the impression, the artist says to himself. *How can one search these shadows? They're great black sheets. It's not the light that softens the scene; it's the darkness hat stamps itself upon the light.*

The artist's face was not the most curious thing about him; the gleam of his pupils slid over the hollow cheeks, while the features remained impassive.

His neighbors raised their heads in their turn.

"That Jacques! He's impossible! One would think that he were happy!"

"It's because he drinks blood," whispered a sheep.

Low as the voice was, Jacques heard it; his ears were as keen as his eyes. His surge of anger made the bunk shake.

"Who said that?" he demanded.

The sheep swallowed his saliva without making any reply.

"Yes, it's true, mate—fresh cable-juice." That from other sheep coming to their comrade's aid. The words were colorless; no one could tell where the hail of insults was coming from.

"Oh, you like it here?"

"So do you, since you stay here," said Jacques, shrugging his shoulders. His anger had faded before these anonymous infamies.

"How can one get out?"

"There's a means."

"What?"

"Death."

"It's cold, is death."

A few hoarse voices approved, though. "No colder than the chain."

"Doesn't everyone cling on to his skin?" said an old man, who was in favor of life.

"It's obvious that you're clinging to yours!"

"Leave us in peace—better to sing, since it's blowing a storm—might as well go on to the end; no one can do any more than that."

"Go on then, lover boy, squeak—if you have the guts."

Jean Hénoe, who had aged ten years in a few months, his back now rounded and his cheeks caved in, coughed and spat, without quitting his horizontal position, and began, quavering like a tinkling bell:

"Does he who loves,
Love,
The knell?"

"Louder! You've got a fine set of pipes, there. Let's hear them."
He continued, almost brazenly:

Does he who blows his nose,
Blow his nose,
Out there?

He's in the ground,
The ground,
A corpse!

Does he who loves,
Love,
The knell?

These incoherent words, to the rhythm of the tocsin, the final ones falling by a semitone, stirred the assembly; with an immense breath, in which revolt was rumbling, they all repeated, in chorus:

Does he who loves,
Love,
The Knell?

The dam had broken; the revolt was in full swing.

The sheep sang with the rest. Some of those wretches took a true part in it, hurling their infamy into the cry of universal vengeance.

It was warm now in the room; the frost on the windows was melting.

There was a shout: "Jacques! Jacques! The carmagnole of the vagabonds!"

The chorus of the song had stirred an echo in their ears.

Coolly, his mordant voice launched into the savage march:

Can you hear it, out there, out there!
It's the old world's knell, at last!
  The knell, the knell, the knell
  The knell, the upheaval!
  In the distance the torch lights up,
The fires and the steel of swords,
  In the distance, the torch is lights up,
The battlefields running red.

Fall away, fall away, iron chains,
Fall away, legends of hell
  Crumble, executioners and kings,
  Power, finance, laws!
  In the distance, the torch lights up,
The battlefields running red,
The fires and the steel of swords.
  In the distance, the torch lights up,
The battlefields running red.

For the seed of the new grain,
Leaves none of the ancient hay,
  The ploughshare is digging deep,

Hollowing out the ground.
In the distance, the torch lights up,
The scythes and the steel of swords.
In the distance the torch light up
The battleground running red.

The red cock crows in the distance,
Now the starvelings rise up.
Covering the whole world,
The perverse world of old.
In the distance, the torch lights up
The scythes and the steel of swords.
In the distance the torch lights up
The battleground running red.

The voices were roaring like a hurricane; it had to be audible outside. A frenzy shook the room.

"Yes, the red cock—let the red cock crow!"

"Do you want that?"

"Yes, there's too much suffering—it has to end! No more cowardice!"

Warm breath escaped their breasts; the air was already on fire when the oath as pronounced.

Who could believe that the idea of death—of such a horrible death—could fill the convicts chained in that room, which would be their pyre, with such grim joy? Those who have seen convict prisons at close range; those, too, who love to turn the knife in their wounds! Imagine an oath sworn in such circumstances, by men who were no longer recognized as having the right to swear it. Well, no one was remiss!

Have you ever seen human tempests? Felt some terrible idea breathing over an agglomeration of men?

Fire! Fire! In the four corners of the prison! Kill them all! Masters and slaves, jailers and prisoners!

Some of the survivors of that day will find a feeble echo of the terrible story here.

Jacques, charges with "setting fire to the cock," as they say, conferred with the others.

The calm with which the convicts got up seemed strange.

The sheep, torn between the fear of selling out their comrades too soon—which would have exposed them to a terrible vengeance—and the desire to fulfill their function, had made a report in which the song took a much larger part than the oath.

There was plenty of time. Conspiracies in a convict prison, given all the difficulties, take months; those that are not thwarted take years to ripen. They were counting on things taking their usual course—but this time, the blood was too hot to wait; circumstances, moreover, lent themselves to it marvelously.

Despair, pushed to its extreme, cannot allow fear to subsist—and what did they have left to fear?

If there are epidemics of disgust, of suicide, it is in places like the hell of the convict prison that they propagate most rapidly; anyone, that day, who had told the convicts that they would be alive in a week's time would have seemed crazy to them.

The wind of revolt was blowing strongly—so strongly that the threat issued by the guards to subject them to the ordinary and extraordinary punishments brought forth a dull growling.

The captive man, like the lion beneath the tamer's whip, sometimes submits for a long time, remaining silent, crawling without complaining—but the whip stings with a more refined insult when it strikes a rawer wound, and the tamer ceases to dominate the wild beast; it rises up and tears apart the man who has outraged it with impunity for so long.

Men are no more cowardly than beasts. The instant before, they are lying down, playing dead before the bestiary; a second later, there they are, standing up, crushing with their weight, tearing with their claws, grinding with their teeth.

Such was the effect of the condemnations, from the cells to the bar of justice, that the administration, via the assembly or the courts, passed against thirty leaders of the revolt.

In the short days of winter, having waited until after lunch to judge more comfortably, the tribunal of the prison had not concluded its sixteenth judgment by nightfall. It made haste, but it was dealing with a revolt! Some of them did not want to respond; others made brief statements that anger launched forth, and time passed—with the result that under the pale lamps of the courtroom, a crowd of convicts, massed like bees on the threshold of the hive, suddenly burst in, and then another, and another—and the courtroom was invaded by a black swarm; the doors were locked and guarded, the accused freed; all in a trice; chains were broken and forced, the whole administration taken prisoner, from the governor to the clerk. The warders, the soldiers and all those sitting in judgment were to be judged in their turn.

The judges' bench was empty.

"Well, Jacques, climb into the chair—we're going to judge them!"

"Me, sit up there! Never—we're going to die with them."

Red and yellow rags were agitating around the prisoners.

"No, it's not necessary to sit up there. That's where the hair's trimmed for Charlot."[21]

"Death plays the violin there."

Jacques was thoughtful, recalling the sessions of his own judgment; he stood there without saying anything.

The anxious prisoners were looking around; now that the convicts were the masters they had calmed down. "What are you going to do?" asked the governor, who was also calm.

"You're going to die with us!" said Jacques. "No one knows what's happened here. The comrades will set it on fire, and the entire prison will go up."

"What do you have against us?" asked the governor.

"You're only instruments, it's true," Jacques replied. "You can't change anything anymore than we can, and others will do what you do so long as the law exists. We're going to die and you'll die with us. It will be an example. We're in despair."

"Me, I wasn't guilty," said Jean Hénoe.

"Me neither," said another.

"It was poverty that made me fall, but no one spared a thought for me except to send me here."

"They only thought of me to put me in the army and condemn me."

Pensively, they expressed their grievances against society, forgetting vengeance."

Outside, no one heard.

"The punishments will be lifted if you let us go," said the governor.

---

[21] A nickname given to the French executioner, after Charles Sanson, who guillotined Louis XVI.

There was an immense burst of laughter. He lowered his white head, no longer finding any answer to make. Indeed, such a promise had already been made in a revolt, but had not been kept—and then again, those in revolt wanted to die."

A spark traversed the courtyard like a shooting star; it was the expected signal.

From his pocket, Jacques took a projectile of the kind that convicts can fabricate no matter what the difficulty: a small tin can, transformed into a bomb. Thrown into the seat of judgment, it set fire to the worm-eaten wood. It was true that they were all going to die together.

Fire flared up elsewhere; from there, they could only see the reflection of the work that was being accomplished in its entirety.

The administrators stared at the convicts, who were all calm.

There was not long to wait. The courtroom burned with a fearful rapidity, the fire licking the walls, reaching the ceiling, spreading a terrible heat through the room; it was a fire that could roast an ox. If there had been any smoke, they would all have choked already, but the worm-eaten wood burned like matches.

At that moment, the clerk remembered an alarm bell of which he had already made use; the button that communicated with it was close by.

The bell, bursting forth frenziedly, summoned help, which began to arrive, for the battle, like the fire, had started on several fronts.

The section of wall to which the tables of the judges' bench had communicated the fire had just collapsed; soldiers broke down the doors in such large numbers that only ten men escaped, beating a retreat toward the wing that offered a haven. The others, taken prisoner, were led back to the cells.

It had required two companies to retake the prison, weapons having come into the hands of the desperate.

Jacques, Pierre and Jean Hénoe were among those who took refuge in the dormitory, not in the hope of surviving but in order not to surrender. They could only defend it on one side.

The commandant who had just retaken the prison arranged his men in the courtyard, and with the fire of machine-guns he set about finishing off the unfortunates, gripped once again by an insensate desire to live.

Have you ever seen human tempests? The fury of repression doubles, or multiplies a hundredfold the strength of each individual. It is the same with those determined to die.

In their retreat, listening to the crackle of the fusillade, the regular sound that machine-guns make as they grind out bullets reminded them of a barbary organ grinding out notes. The sinister tolling of the tocsin announced the revolt; the cannon in the harbor counted the quarter-hours of the crisis with its booming shots. It was terrible. They all said to themselves: *Any of us who survives will be a vile coward.*

Jacques remembered that the pharmacy was underneath the building, and that the fire would spread to its inflammable essences. Nothing would save them if they could hasten the spread of the fire.

This time, it was Jean Hénoe who furnished the match; he took an old tinder-box from the lining of his rags and a wad of tinder, which a recently-deceased veteran had given to him. "He had a funny idea, the fellow who gave me this, saying: 'it might come in handy.' It will, indeed."

It served so well that the red cock was soon beating its wings above them. The roof burned with a terrible crackle.

There was no other means of preventing the fire from spreading than isolating the building. That was what was done.

The air, the sea breeze and the land breeze blew over the ocean of flames; the ardent tongues undulated like the ears in a wheat-field.

From the waves, winds and flames rose a nameless chorus, to which the flames engulfed in the chimneys that were still standing provided an organ-like accompaniment.

Jacques had a strange stroke of luck. He was standing on his own in a corner of the dormitory that was free of the fire. From that shelter, from which he would not emerge, the sculptor gazed, all eyes, and listened, all ears, to the monstrous choir singing, and the harps of the wind made the air quiver, larding it with wrath.

The booming note of the alarm canon and the plaint of the tocsin were still accentuating the desolate melody.

In the sky, the fire sent the redness of the morning far and wide, while fringes of shadow floated like those of the polar auroras.

The ear grasps tones that are scarcely sensible in scales: from scales extending over enormous distances, Jacques filled all his senses with the art of the imminent future. For a long time he gazed at and listened to the scene he thought he would never see and the song he thought he would never sing.

The poem of hatred germinated in love; destruction saluted its birth.

Suddenly, the pharmacy exploded. A bouquet of fireworks rose up toward he clouds.

The section of wall supporting the sculptor collapsed, with the rest of the shell, into the sea. Men fell into the water; several were rescued.

Death did not want Jacques.

Jean Hénoe, dreaming in his infirmary bed, his face covered in cotton wool, said that liberty must be a beautiful thing for him to have forgotten La Greluchette. What he forgot, most of all, was that an exemplary punishment awaited him once he was discharged from the infirmary. But such is the attachment to life that a man who narrowly escapes death rarely attempts it a second time. There are even some who begin to find it good that Death has slammed the door in their face. Such was the case with Jean Hénoe.

Jacques said nothing; he was thinking about something else.

When the invalids had healed, Jacques—whose death-sentence was commuted—Pierre and Jean Hénoe, who were all to be deported to New Caledonia, were put on the same ship. The doctor who had cared for them declared that Pierre's survival was a curious case, from a scientific viewpoint.

A long time after the departure of the ship carrying them, Jacques' group of the future was exhibited as a specimen of criminal art, along with Lacenaire's verses. [22]

---

[22] The murderer Pierre Lacenaire, executed in 1836, wrote his memoirs and a great deal of poetry while in jail before and after receiving his death sentence, representing his crimes as a protest against social injustice. He contrived to make himself famous, exercising an influence on Honoré de Balzac's account of the human comedy and allegedly providing the inspirational seed of Dostoyesky's *Crime and Punishment*.

XIII. Eleazer

Roll was able to dispense with his frankness on the subject of Dr. Martiali's séances. Soon after their reportage in the newspapers, the scholarly doctor had clandestinely transported that which he did not want to destroy or expose to judiciary curiosity to the shop of Eleazer, merchant of curiosities—who was none other than himself.

Madame Tristan, the "protectress" of little Gertrude, followed her husband's example. Nothing more was heard of Dr. Martiali's séances. The clientele to whom Madame Tristan had thought of offering Gertrude, as fresh as a May rose, along with her faded bouquets, did not see the old woman again. Her boutique, where various object—always the same ones-were displayed was closed one morning, with a notice that no one contested: *Closed Because of Death.*

It required a certain boldness to put up such a notice, but Madame Tristan's clients had no desire to attract attention. As for the owner, he had been paid a month in advance; the last one still had four days to run—and anyway, he was a foreigner. When had Madame Tristan died, then? A few old women wondered—but no one could answer. Who the Devil could have guessed that Madame Tristan was Madame Eleazer?

Eleazer's shop was situated in the Marais, in a house with an enormous courtyard that formed a corner with the Rue Pavée. The curiosity-merchant's clients were of several kinds: scholars, artists, collectors and maniacs. All of them, thanks to his marvelous erudition, held him in great esteem; a few were enthusiasts. With clients like that, Eleazer earned a tolerable living and satisfied his literary tastes.

He had one other class of clients: they were borrowers, a sorry breed, whom he treated with the utmost rigor.

Madame Eleazer's clientele was the same, at a different level of intelligence, as Madame Tristan's. La Tristan sold fresh meat to bourgeois gluttons; La Eleazer sold the enjoyment of the dead to sophisticates of archaeological debauchery.

That evening, there was a private committee-meeting in the home of the worthy spouses. Little Gertrude, transported like the other objects, had been drugged for the circumstance; it was the same intoxication into which, according to Eleazer, fakirs passed before being buried alive.

He alone could wake the child up, and he did not want to wake her right away.

They could not leave in the other house anything that might awaken suspicion; it was necessary to get rid of it in a sure and profitable manner; that is what we are about to witness.

A table covered by a white cloth is placed in the third room. Eleazer has just brought the evening to a close by putting the child to sleep by means of a few magnetic passes.

The woman is tall and gaunt, with a tower of black hair on her viperfish skull, beneath an elegant hat that renders her cruel round eyes more hideous. Her lips are thin; her tongues darts words charged with venom.

The man is hideous and handsome at the same time, according to the circumstances in which he appears.

In the morning, his skull-cap on his head, enveloped in an old dressing-gown in which he almost disappears,

Eleazer, his spectacles fixed on his hooked nose, studies endless calculations in his enormous books. One might take him for a mummy, so parchment-like is his skin. He has the laughter and tears of a crocodile as he calculates the profit or loss of the previous day. If he is in deficit, woe betide anyone who comes within his reach. If he has made a tidy profit, Eleazer will shave his victims even more closely, the bird of prey being tempted.

The Eleazer who treats artists and scholars as equals, more inspired than the former and more erudite than the latter, throws away the cap that conceals his immense skull; he invents; he tells stories; he argues, sometimes with a bitter softness, sometimes raising his voice, informing the scholars and dazzling the poets. Then, he is dominant; he is the Djaina Sarma.

That evening, he was neither one of those transformations; he wore the mask of the sphinx; he was seeking.

The child having gone to sleep between them, Eleazer slowly concludes his passes. The child is sleeping profoundly; there is no danger of her waking up. It is in that state that she will respond to questions before the old man encountered by his wife takes her away, to do with her as he wishes, or Eleazer saves her.

There's no reason to fear! There are thousands of disappearances that no one notices. So many people occupy no more space than animals that one throws into the water sooner or later.

Eleazer takes the child's hand.

"Can you answer me?"

A plaint escapes Gertrude's lips.

"What are you thinking about?"

The dreaming child repeats—whether by chance or not—what Madame Eleazer's clients say: "You turn fresh flowers into a dungheap."

"Well, no, not this time," says Eleazer

"Bah!" replies the old lady, uncovering her teeth, which bite her dull lips. "One might as well entrust a mouse to a cat as the innocence of a child to the vicomte."

"I've found her a refuge."

"Are you going to go back on the deal?"

"You know the village of Russian legend in which cocks don't crow and the inhabitants never wake up—that's where I want to send her."

"What if the man back out of the deal?"

"We've promised him Gertrude; death will break the deal. If he's not content, let him complain." Taking the child's hand, he says: "Answer me, Gertrude—I want you to answer me. What do you see?"

"Total darkness!"

He pours a few drops of liquid into a spoon and slides it through the child's lips. Her body shivers.

"What is there around you? Come on, answer me."

"Nothing!"

A deeper breath lifts up her breast; indeed, there is no longer anything.

"You're mad, Eleazer," says the old woman.

"I carry out experiments; I've woken up sleepers with the right dose; now I want to wake someone dead. I've found the liquid that conserves human bodies; I think I have the one that wakes them up, as water revives a rotifer desiccated by the sun."

Someone rang the front doorbell. Carefully closing the two rooms at the back, Eleazer went to open it.

It was the vicomte—which is to say, the old eccentric we have seen in the café in the Place Clichy, in company with the "mionette."

"Well?"

"Come in."

"The child's here?"

"Yes."

The old man introduced the vicomte into the room where Madame Eleazer, continuing to bite her lip, was watching the child, who was sitting inert with her arms folded, her head leaning on the back of the chair.

The child had been decorated for the occasion, her unbound hair covering her shoulders, a red dress contrasting with her pallor.

For a few moments the vicomte remained standing, looking at Gertrude, drinking her in with his eyes. Finally, he took out a wallet. "Count it," he said.

That is what the old woman did, with a certain dexterity.

"It's all here."

"Now, how are we going to take her away."

"That's easy," Eleazer replied. "I've arranged everything—but we need to wait for an hour. Please sit down, Monsieur le Vicomte. You've come alone, haven't you?"

"Do you think I'd be imprudent enough to bring anyone with me?"

"That would indeed have been imprudent, and for my part, I'd no longer be following your orders."

"Well, Master Scholar," said the vicomte, shrugging his shoulders at the foolish notion that the other had of his prudence, "what have we been doing today?"

"Among other things, I've been seeking the elixir of youth."

"And have you found it?"

"Almost. The beauty of the features doesn't come back with my liquor, but the strength is greater than at any other epoch of life. I'll find the freshness of the face in time."

The vicomte smiled at his future youth.

"You're incredulous? It's no more difficult than putting to sleep or waking up."

"Indeed—and this is the second time that I'll be able to appreciate your talents in that respect."

"Would you like to sample the elixir?"

The vicomte was apprehensive, but there remained from his heritage a pride withered into vanity, an audacity transformed into boastful conceit, and he did not want to recoil.

"Let's try it," he said.

Eleazer took a red bottle and poured the liquid into the vicomte's glass without stirring it. Then he shook the bottle violently.

"My wife and I," he said, "will take a dose of the elixir that would kill you, not being habituated to it."

The liquid had, in fact, turned brown. It was a counter-elixir that Eleazer had mixed in thoroughly.

With a slight flutter of his heart, the vicomte picked up his glass. "To beauty!" he said, raising it with an ape-like smile addressed to Gertrude.

With a wink, Eleazer made his worthy wife drink without further hesitation.

"Well," said the merchant of curiosities, "don't you feel the blood running more rapidly in your veins?"

The vicomte was still sitting down. He put both hands to his breast, where the blood-flow was, in fact, ebbing.

"A few more moments," said Eleazer, in reply to the mute interrogation of the decrepit sensualist..

Another few moments, and the vicomte was sleeping the same slumber as Gertrude—or the same death, if Eleazer could not wake them up.

"Eudoxia," said Eleazer, "light my way while I transport my subjects to the sarcophagi. I bought them this morning expressly for this purpose."

"There were, indeed, two curious Egyptian sarcophagi in a back cellar. He opened them, deposited the vicomte's body in the larger one and laid Gertrude down carefully in the smaller one; and, without forgetting to place footstools beneath their heads, he closed them carefully and took away the key of the back cellar, where they would remain until he recalled them to life.

XIV. The Testimony of the Dead

Roll had soon finished with his first fit of humanity; he was able to extract his bleeding heart from his breast and become marble once again. Love had taken hold of him momentarily, but he did not want to suffer it any longer.

With Anna dead, everything was dead. What he wanted now was science. He seemed to have accomplished his ambition, to have incorporated his life. Anna was a dream! Had he not always felt the desire, the fatal necessity of combining the two monsters into one?

Finally, all those monstrous ideas ceased; calm took possession of Roll; he devoted himself to the affairs that were entrusted to him with a marvelous lucidity.

Sometimes, in the midst of his judiciary preoccupations, he thought of the scant value of evidence, and laughed at human stupidity. He was inclined, however, to tip the scales in favor of justice. Was that caprice?

One day, when he had surpassed himself in the case of two children who had been victims of the cupidity of a parent, Roll had established the instruction on bases so unassailable that the public ministry had nothing more to do than impose the most severe sentence. The defense lawyer scarcely dared to mention extenuating circumstances; the accused was thunderstruck.

Suddenly, a woman clad in rags, dragging two children after her, about four or five years old, launched herself toward the tribunal.

Roll recognized Anna: Anna, who, in order to escape the horrible obsession of her love, had come to demand justice.

Her children would not be soiled, she thought, and Philippe would be avenged, avenged on love, avenged on her.

"What do you want?" asked the president.

"Justice! Justice!"

The word justice, every time it is pronounced by the desperate, evokes the idea of madness.

"Explain yourself," said the president.

Explain herself? She tried, but it would have necessary to say everything at once. She began: "My husband has been murdered."

"Has that any relevance to the case before the court?"

"No, Monsieur, but it concerns one of the judges here present."

Like the others, Roll stared at the woman who was speaking with a frightful calmness.

"Address yourself to him at an appropriate time; it's impossible in the middle of another trial."

"But he's the one who is the murderer—the murder of Philippe Wolff, my husband."

The entire tribunal rose to its feet. Philippe Wolff, as everyone knew and could see, was there; there was no possible doubt as to the unfortunate woman's madness.

Thus, Anna was taken to the prison hospital. That was the worst turn that destiny had in reserve for Roll, for, buried as Anna was in the lunatic asylum to which she was about to be taken, some unexpected circumstance might occur that would lend substance to her terrible accusations.

A summary investigation proved that the woman who had demanded justice was not Madame Wolff at all, since she lived in Argenteuil and was named d'Erfel. It was under that name that an old man, presumably her father or her husband, had rented an isolated house or her near the boulevard to the railway station.

Her story was simple; one night, jumping through a window that had been found broken, she had carried off her children and thrown herself with them into the Seine. Some distance away, young men returning from one of those meetings that so displeased Jacques' judges, had pulled her out almost dead, having let herself drift with her children in her arms.

Confided to the mother of one of her rescuers, Ana hovered between life and death for a long time; her mind had surely gone astray, she said so many strange things. One day, she had left the good woman in order to go to the court. That was all that was known.

There was no need to seek any further; it was perfectly clear. The two children, for whom the country air had done a great deal of good, were sent to La Chylokière, to which André had recently been recommitted.

All was going well.

Roll, meanwhile, experiencing a disagreeable impression every time he presented himself at a trial, had himself appointed, in his capacity as a scientist, as director of a scientific mission whose purpose was to investigate the laws of people still living in a state of nature.

XV. The Sacrifice

In addition to the agreeable pastime of trying on his subjects, for whom no one would come in search to his home, the fakirs' secret of inhumation and resurrection; and in addition to the various methods coming to him from the same source, some in order not to put anything into his stomach for various lengths of time, others to do the opposite; Eleazer was investigating all the knowledge of India and Egypt, deciphering ancient writings with an amazing facility.

That evil genius reported to him knowledge of the past and the present; he hung over that encyclopedia like a spider in its web.

Sacrifices inspired an ardent curiosity in him, like Roll's desire to become his brother. By virtue of cheating the Parcae of Colombes by means of mysterious rites, he had hallucinated himself, and had passed from the mysteries of science to the fantastical of dreams, from genius to madness. That is why, after the sacrifice of Pékian, he thought of leading the three deluded women voluntarily to sacrifice one of themselves. Now that the mystery of the sleep and reawakening of fakirs was, he thought, about to yield a response, he would give himself the spectacle of a voluntary sacrifice, to search and examine in depth that supreme act, in which a human being was completely annihilated, in order no longer to be anything but a will dominating dolor.

Eleazer would have liked to observe the difference between mystical sacrifice and social sacrifice, but as the revolutionaries who throw their life into some enterprise for which one never emerges usually choose their confidant carefully or do not have one—which is better—he could only hope for that second experiment.

Remarkably, those whom science leads into madness have the avidity of crows; they strip to the bones those whom they circle around; thus Eleazer circled around the house on the Colombes road.

The three women were not exempt from that avidity themselves; their dwelling, a veritable magpie's nest, was overflowing with provisions of money and heaped-up things. It was in that lumber-room that Karpa, Holda and Nara were dreaming, with one paw on a sack of coins and the other on the bards' harp.

It is strange that the individuals of our fin-de-siècle are either sketches in clay that shatter in the furnaces or figures of bronze that take on superb form. The greatest things are perverted into crimes or transfigured into marvelous gifts.

In the House of the Lord, they were perverted into crimes—which did not prevent the poor people of the neighborhood from coming in search of their usual pittance, nor insolvent travelers from sleeping there in the small lodgings of the right wing, under the surveillance of the great God of the woods, who was very inoffensive, and the gardener, who was no less inoffensive.

Irresponsible, to the extent that an oyster might be, the gardener Thomas continued not to pass over the parvis of the Temple, on which he came to deposit that evening—a Saturday at the end of January—five or six dishes he had prepared. He was also the cook; those dishes were very appetizing, as he knew by virtue of having tasted them. Having out down the dishes, carefully covered, Thomas went to the rooms overlooking the garden.

Two female travelers were installed there that evening, one blonde, the other brunette, both with haggard eyes. Thin and tall, they were almost the same type—that which gives great pains and great misery.

With the mistrust that they had acquired at their own expense, the two women were inspecting the place where necessity had forced them to take shelter, and inspecting one another; each one found in her chance companion a distraught expression; they were both right.

Both fugitives, the good or bad luck that brought them together inspired each of them with dread. Everything, for them, might be a trap.

Thomas had a discretion that recommended him to place the two travelers' food on a table, and then retire.

Neither one was hungry, but they sat down, perhaps out of commiseration for one another, and took a little nourishment. Each kept her secret, but the suspicion faded away.

Finally, drawing upon ancient memories, the brunette said timidly to the other: "I once met a person who resembled you sufficiently to be mistaken for you, in very sad circumstances. Don't you remember it?"

The other sought for a long time in silence, and found in the pauperess a vague resemblance to someone glimpsed in a very different time.

"I went to ask a judge for his protection, to save my child. It was his wife who received me; it's her that you resemble."

The other shivered; she remembered, but did not reply.

A horrible scream brought them to their feet.

Wasn't that a murder? Does every name lie? Was the House of the Lord, perhaps a house of crime?

Doubtless by virtue of Thomas's error, the door was not locked; they went through it and found themselves in the garden.

A window illuminated as if by fire opened a bay of flame; it was from there that the cry had come.

The window was not very high; the two women could look in, if the stronger lent the other her shoulders. That was what they did, in the silence of terror.

The blonde, hoisted on to her companion's shoulders, supported the sight of what was happening in the lighted room without uttering a cry, and then touched the other to tell her to take her place.

The latter, in the same silence, climbed up in her turn.

What they saw was terrible.

In the middle of the room, on a stove open at the top, it was no longer pigeons that were fanning the flame with their crazed wings, nor the red goat-kid bleating miserably, but the youngest of the three women, engulfed in the immense opening up to her waist, attached by an iron chain, writhing in the midst of agonies that had drawn a frightful scream from her. With a death-rattle in her throat, she was trying to respond to the song of a sort of phantom, who was waving a torch with her raised arms and tranquilly reciting a rhythmic monologue:

O fire born of the sun,
O fire that purifies,
Devour vermilion blood.
O fire take this life!

Sap runs in the flame
Like the blood on the pyre;

The heart beats in the flame
Where death is about to pass.

To these incoherent words the frightened voices of two old women responded. One might have thought it the psalmody of Tenebrae in a Catholic church.

The unfortunate secured in the flames shivered for the last time. The fire had reached her heart.

Terrified, the two pauperesses searched around the walls for a way out, which they did not find. Night enveloped the house. They wandered, fearful of the sound of their footsteps. They helped one another, united by the common terror.

What could they do? No exit! Like a beast in a cage, they repeated their circuit of the walls.

As they went past a low window they saw the gardener, by the glow of a night-light, profoundly asleep. On the night-light a cup of mulled wine was warming gently, awaiting his awakening.

That awakening was not to be soon, for the fellow was sleeping as deeply as one does in a tomb. The house could have been consumed by fire, as the victim had been consumed, but Thomas would not have woken up.

Sometimes, fear will grow, taking hold of the entire being, shaking it with a horrible frisson all the way to the ends of the hair.

A few hours seemed to them an eternity; covered in cold sweat, they circled again and again, always between the walls and the trees—which, raising their desolate branches, took on spectral forms in the shadows. They wandered in that fashion all night.

In the morning, from a distance, they saw Thomas opening the entry door, rubbing his eyes. They ran out fearfully and disappeared into the fields.

"Well!" said Thomas. "Are they mad, those two?" And he shrugged his shoulders tranquilly. "Oh well, they aren't very polite. Lodge people comfortably, and they don't even say thank you! And yet, they must have slept well—the beds are soft, thank God! One sinks into the feathers there."

On going into the travelers' room, however, he perceived that the beds had not been touched.

The Djaina had also left the House of the Lord early, thinking that he knew nothing more, and wondering whether Gilles de Rais, who had cut the throats of little children, had discovered any more. Then, utterly mad and perfectly calm, he went to catch a train at the nearest railway station, in order to return to the house in the Rue Pavée.

He went down into the back cellar and lifted the lids of the sarcophagi. Gertrude, who was pale, seemed to be asleep. The vicomte had taken on a livid tint, and the acrid odor that escaped from the sarcophagus filled the cellars.

Eleazer went back upstairs, thoughtfully. He had given the vicomte too strong a dose.

Eudoxia had to enlighten her husband again. The putrefying corpse was buried deeply enough to avoid any "unpleasantness," as Madame Eleazer put it, but the odor spread outside, rising through an air-vent into the street.

"It's Père Cachemuche's butchery that smells like that," said a housewife, pinching her nose in front of the garlands of sausages.

"Eh? What's that you're saying?" cried the fat man, who had advanced, thinking that he had a customer, and had heard the words. "Which of you is slandering my shop? It's you who stink like that!"

"Old rogue! You'll see whether it's us if we take your threadworms to be analyzed at the municipal laboratory."

"Threadworms yourselves!"

And the old man slammed his door with that scornful insult, while the two ladies went on their way, their handkerchiefs over their noses, as far as the tripe-shop, hesitating over which of the two establishments had the more unsupportable odor.

"It's here for sure—the old fool was right; it's coming from here, that reek of death."

It was indeed, the reek of death, but the pork-butcher, as the good women said, was entirely innocent.

XVI. La Chylokière

A benevolent individual had spent two or three million founding an agricultural colony at La Chylokière, for those orphans who seemed to have a strong constitution, where the little detainees were employed in agricultural labor. The generous benefactress' property being immense, there were never too many arms there, and Providence seemed to have spread its gifts in profusion upon the pious house, for a generous philanthropist had doubled its millions in a few years—although it is true that that was partly for him.

The work done by the children, who get up at four o'clock in the morning—spending little time at meals and even less in study—brings in much more than the breeding of the flocks. There are also naïve individuals pious souls will well-lined purses. Thus is it that La Chlyolière invades more and more of the surrounding lands.

A few small foundlings whose young age did permit them to be of as much use as the bigger ones were the object of the solicitude of the aforementioned pious souls, the board and lodging of the brats being charged at between twenty and forty francs a month.

Two very small ones had just arrived; shrewd for their age, they liked nothing better than telling the others incredible stories—for example, that there was a Red Room in their house, where they had been afraid of the wind; that their father was no longer good, as he had once been; and that they could not say any more because they were too frightened.

The poor little mites asked for their mother, weeping abundantly. It was necessary to put them in a separate building, what they said being capable of doing considerable wrong to Philippe Wolff, whose honorability no one doubted.

The two children were thus placed with a young vagabond named André, designated particularly for administrative severity, who was not allowed out of the cell where he prepared the wool for long, and could not repeat the disordered words of the two little ones.

Where, then, could the plaints of the poor innocents have gone? Their mother had, it's true, escaped from the madhouse, but how could she have got them back? As for the family on the paternal side, Roll had disowned them. Anna was an orphan and only had distant relatives. The children had, therefore, to forget their early years; from now on they belonged to that terrible stepmother known as public charity.

There are two sides to everything; their arrival in André's company had been a joy for the latter.

"Don't think of dong them any harm," said the warder, as he pushed the tearful children into his cell. "They can card wool—that will amuse them, and I'd better find this evening that they've done as much as you!" And he went out.

"Where do you kids come from?" André asked, sitting them down in the wool scattered around him.

The younger one, Charlot, wiping the tears from his eyes with his sleeve, already reassured, raised his bright eyes to look at André. "From home! But we mustn't say so, or they'll beat us again."

"Where is this home?"

"Where the Red Room was."

That kid has little suns in his peepers, André thought.

The elder, reassured in his turn, said: "They took Mama away because she said that Papa wasn't Papa—that he had killed him in order to be him."

"She's mad, your poor Mama."

"That's what they said, but I know it's not so."

"Poor kid! Are you going to work?"

"No," was the response of Charlot and the well-named Loulou.

"Then I'll have to do it all, or you'll be beaten black and blue."

"That makes no difference," said Charlot. "We've already been beaten!"

André established them more warmly in the woolen debris.

What a pity they're already cracked, like the mother! he said to himself, as he calmed the children. Then, in memory of Gertrude, his little friend, whom he would never see again, two warm tears rose up from his heart.

"No," he said, "I can't cry; there'd be a flow greater than the Seine if I started to cry!"

Quickly, with his short fingers, already hardened and swollen by the work, André started carding furiously.

Then the little ones tried to do the same, until their red hands were scratches all over. That put them to sleep.

"No matter how miserable one is, the sandman passes just the same, and that's good," said André, philosophically.

The task having been complete easily, the quota was doubled the following day. That was the everyday torture.

"This evening," André said to the little ones, "the sandman will come." They consoled themselves thus.

By virtue of questioning the children, André too had ended up believing that he mother was mad.

XVII. The Wolf Emerges from the Woods

Starved of science, thirsty for love, unable to inspire anything but hatred, condemned by concern for his safety to bury his crime under other crimes, like a cadaver beneath the earth, Roll no longer quit his study, digging through and raking over human miseries with his wolf's claws. Then, utterly weary of investigations in which evidence was too easily accumulated against the innocent or guilty, the letter written to his brother by the doctor in the Boulevard Clichy, who had never been found, echoed in his head. While awaiting the departure of the scientific mission, he became so obsessed by that letter that he spent hours on end running his eyes over Martiali's lines, his thoughts suspended.

To be sure, an intelligent man would not have been able to carry out Roll's crimes without being in a morbid state of mind. In fact, his overexcited imagination gave an intense acuity to his perceptions; he sensed the emanation of the piece of paper; he saw the person who had written it, his broad forehead as yellow and polished as a death's-head, his follow eyes and his pug nose.

One evening, half by intuition and half by hazard, he discovered the shop of curiosities in the Rue Pavée and went in, drawn by an indefinable attraction.

The frightful odor, instead of dissipating, was still rising up in spite of the vicomte's interment, but as pastilles of seraglio incense were burning incessantly in the shop and the cellars, people searched everywhere in the street except for the place where the corpse as rotting.

From the pork-butcher's shop and the tripe-shop a pile of sausages, hams and tripe had been thrown into the gutter; stray dogs and cats were having a feast every evening; they were so persistent that it was only necessary to give them a few blows with the hook to kill two or three of them.

The most ardent in complaining about the bad smell were Eleazer and his wife. All the petitions to the Prefecture of Police to make enquires about the infection of the street commenced with the complaints of the two worthy spouses.

Roll, finding himself unexpectedly confronted by Eleazer, recognized his man; this had to be Martiali—although neither the dwelling nor he profession were similar, it had to be him.

Eleazer thought that he was in the presence of Philippe, but, not sensing his personality, thought about the strange adventure of the trial at which Anna had appeared in mid-hearing.

She was right, he thought. *This isn't Philippe!*

Roll, for his part, temporized. "My dear Monsieur Eleazer," he said—the name was on the sign—"would you be kind enough to let me have the works of Paracelsus? He was one of the first magnetizers wasn't he? His works are well-known to the celebrated Martiali."

"Indeed—but there's also Van Helmont; they were Mesmer's precursors."

"Do you believe in all that?"

"There's truth and falsehood in everything. I'm not a doctrinarian, merely a seeker."

"Just like me—that's why, I spite of the experiments carried out and repeated, the word belief may be replaced by the word doubt; nothing is yet demonstrated."

"That's perfectly true."

They talked, observing one another, not thinking about their words, which took flight at hazard.

That was all, for the first conversation—but Roll came back, bringing the old books that he had requested, and asking for others. He came back repeatedly. He had conceived for Eleazer the hatred that he had had for his brother—a hatred that would only be extinguished by the merchant's death.

Roll was dealing with a strong adversary. Eleazer scented the wolf, and the current of hatred between those two savage natures, that would fatally bear away one or the other.

They struggled, slyly, not wishing to question one another, diving, sniffing the effluvia in the air, each trying, in the secrecy of his will-power, to break the other.

Is it really possible that there are things of that kind? Are they not all madmen, from the fakirs to the two of them? Such was the question that Roll eternally asked himself; fatality cut through it without resolving it.

Eudoxia, who was nostalgic for her role as Madame Tristan, having found an opportunity to reopen the bargain boutique for fresh flesh, absented herself on a daily basis—which Roll had noticed.

"My dear Monsieur Eleazer," he said, during one of these absences, looking at him with his bright eyes, "do you know that there's a conclusive experiment that you and I could carry out to determine the truth about the famous magnetic fluid, about which we talk like blind men reasoning about colors."

"What experiment?" Eleazer tried to stare Roll down. The latter held his gaze.

The two monsters were face to face; the street was deserted; Eudoxia would be late back. Roll knew that, having studied hr comings and goings. He went to the door, turned the key and put it in his pocket.

"My dear Master, we're going to try to magnetize one another."

Fear and the certainty of his crimes paralyzed Eleazer more than Roll's magnetic power.

Have you seen acrobats fall when they lose their equilibrium? Thus will-power escaped Eleazer, and Roll, like a tamer mastering a beast, fascinated him.

Eleazer was vanquished; the Djaina Sarma had found his master.

Roll did not know himself that he had that power of will, converted into brutal force, to such a high degree.

"Where does the fetid odor of this street come from?" he asked the paralyzed merchant.

Eleazer did not rely, turning his head away to flee his enemy's eyes.

Roll repeated the question. Sensing that he was lost, the other seized the lamp and threw it at his enemy; it did not hit him, but the floor was covered in blazing oil. The two wild beasts threw themselves upon one another, biting and clawing, drawing blood with their fingernails and teeth.

The struggle was brief; Roll strangled the Djaina as he had strangled Diane, and then slowly, in the midst of the flames that were beginning to fill the room, put the key back into the lock. Lowering his hat over his face, he slipped away, while the neighbors, perceiving the flames, raised the alarm.

When the first was partly extinct the charred body of the antiquary was pulled out, and Madame Eleazer, coming back from her own shop, discovered the disaster.

The worthy spouse of the Djaina disappeared without seeking further information. She was never seen again; she had no need to go back, her other shop offering her security. She did not leave without regretting the savings that Eleazer had amassed, but life comes before everything else.

Just as the fire seemed to be going out, the chemical products accumulated in the shop exploded. The conflagration was not brought under control until the following day; the building, of which nothing remained but the walls, had been isolated

Of Eleazer's body and those of the two men who had brought it out of the shop nothing remained but charred bones, but when the rubble was searched the curiosities in the cellars were discovered absolutely intact. In the third, the two Egyptian sarcophagi—one open, one closed—with holes in the lids, as if to permit respiration, attracted particular attention.

Then there was excitement—a poignant emotion—for the child lying in the smaller of the sarcophagi appeared to be not dead but cataleptic; such was the opinion of the physicians.

The mystery of the Rue Pavée impassioned the crowd for a long time—even longer than Gertrude's awakening. Thanks to the impression produced by the intense heat of the conflagration, her blood had naturally resumed the circulation of life without the assistance of any secret of the fakirs—if the languor from which there seemed to be no hope that she would ever emerge could be called life.

Scarcely had she raised her head than she fell back on the pillow; doubtless she would die without ever having been able to speak.

From time to time a spoonful of cordial was introduced between her lips, without receiving any sign of consciousness; her mind must have given way.

The presence of Gertrude in Eleazer's cellar constituted what was called the Mystery of the Rue Pavée. It was soon supplemented by the Colombes Mystery, without anyone suspecting that the two were connected.

The remains of the holocausts over which the two old ladies had so often prayed and wept while singing the Djaina's hymns, doubtless attaining the heavens, eventually attracted the attention of the neighbors, and a raid by the police discovered, not the truth, but a few remains of the voluntary victim. The two madwomen and the gardener Thomas were sentenced to life with hard labor.

This time Roll was not one of the judges; he had departed. Perhaps he had seen some danger, apart from his dead enemy, in a longer sojourn in Paris.

XVIII. The Cyclones

The launch of the commandant of the Ducos Peninsula, manned by convicts in order to go to Lifou to pick up a cargo of rosewood, did not return on that occasion, two of the bold transportees having threatened to throw the other two into the sea if they did not consent to the escape. All four had set forth; they rowed as hard as they could in order to get as far away as possible before the alarm was raised; it would have cost them their lives had they been caught, for they would have defended themselves.

The weather was dull—not a breath of wind—and the sea calm. They knew that that kind of calm presages a cyclone, and they were in the epoch when one was bound to occur—every third year. The escapees also knew that for several years, during each of those torments, a whaler had been seen gliding over the waves, like the legendary Flying Dutchman.

That ship without a flag was said to be haunted by the dead. It was called the Phantom Ship. What if they could board it? The legend had been repeated for a long time, everyone laughing at it; it was easy, in thinking about it in bright moonlight, to assume an appearance of unbelief. No one demanded that ships display their colors during cyclones.

Cyclones are marriages with death; the pale bride extends her banner of lightning over the waves; the elements croak the wedding march with frightful squalls.

The waves eat the earth and night eats the waves, said Andia, the bard of Atai.[23] Is it the vessel that sinks or the land that is swallowed up?

The four desperate men manning the commandant's launch were not frightened of the darkness or the wrath of the elements; it was liberty for them, for dying is also being set free, liberated in the dreamless sleep. The two who had be forced to take part in the expedition kept quiet, finding the adventure good and trying, like everyone else in the lands of cyclones, to believe that not all those who whirl in their vertigo-haunted waltzes are doomed.

Like autumn leaves in whirlwinds, launches, brigs and schooners dance, colliding like nutshells in the harbor, where the alarm gun punctuates the tempest, trying to orientate themselves.

Everything was black; an immense flash of lightning tearing through the shadow displayed two vessels in the distance, over the deep, like two frightened birds flying madly, chased by the torment.

Have you ever heard the strident music of the wind? The breaking of forests, the howling of the tempest? In the furious concert of nature, one senses the universal harmony.

Jacques had one heard a distant echo of that bardsong it in the flames of a blaze.

---

[23] Atai was one of the chiefs who led the native revolt in New Caledonia while Louis Michel was a prisoner there; in the book she subsequently wrote about the songs and folklore of the canaques she mentions Andia as a dwarf member of Atai's tribe, who played the role of storyteller. But for that single mention and this passing reference, he would have lived and died unnoticed by history.

In that formidable racket, who would even have thought of showing a flag?

They would no longer be searching for the escaped convicts; the launch would be in peril, that was all; they would regret the launch and perhaps the men too, for they were intelligent and good workers. It must have been that vessel, dancing out there with a larger one. When the first lightning-flash, which had displayed them in the sea and the waves, was succeeded by a second, only the large hull remained; it was devoid of a mast, like a monstrous scarab with its wing-cases closed.

In the prison colony, the name of the launch was inscribed among those of lost vessels, and the men aboard were added to the list of the dead.

That was an error; the men had boarded the brig, which let itself go for a long time in the waltz of the wind, and emerged victoriously. The tempest being in decline, suddenly deploying its mast, it glided away within view of the harbor, heading south. The torment had passed in the harbor; the ships were shaking the ends of their broken yard-arms, still bobbing at anchor. In the town there were no more roofs; they had taken off like immense white butterflies, borne away by the wind.

The water ran in torrents into the sea, covered with the green hair of uprooted mangroves. Not the least avid for the spectacle were the members of a scientific mission which had arrived the day before to record the systems of justice employed by the primitives. Those learned travelers were lucky, especially the director of the mission, for never had a more savage being contemplated a more terrible spectacle with his bestial eyes.

During voyages, Roll Wolff quivered with the furious electricity of his being.

The last scene of the tempest had been magnificent; now nature, calmed down, as lowering the curtain.

Roll, who had been gripped by the beauty of the spectacle, especially the unchained effluvia, had lived the tempest, the cyclone; it was the magnification of his life.

Was it his fault if his mother had caused the effluvia of that fantastic battle of wild beasts to pass into him? Was it his fault that he had been thrown into the net that possessed him with the madness of murder? In brighter weather, Roll had encountered other currents, with the result that he was an enormous but poorly-equilibrated force rolling along, crushing everything in its passage.

Roll went back to the governor's mansion, where he dined in the company of the scientists in his entourage; the latter could not do otherwise than to lead the conversation to the glorious judiciary past of Philippe Wolff, who had been famous long before the governor's departure for Noumea; it would be agreeable to his guest to know that nowhere were the services that he had rendered unknown. Now it was the turn of science; Philippe Roll was a universal man!

Philippe's name rang false in Roll's ears. The tempest had exchanged so much electricity with him that his nerves were saturated by it. He changed the subject, but his intention served him badly. Like the needle of a compass, which is crazed by cyclones, seeking in vain for north, Roll's instinct sought and sought without finding.

"Do you know," he asked, "what that cockleshell was that the other cockleshell, your launch, ran into so politely?"

"It was the Phantom Brig; it passes by, it's said, during cyclones."

"What? There are such legends here? I believe that the explanation was adapted to the appearance of the ship."

"To the appearance and the fact; every three years the brig passes through the cyclone; it's the third time it has been seen—the second for me."

"Doesn't it pass within canon-range?"

"Yes, very nearly."

"Well?"

"I don't see why one should fire on ships during a tempest; then again, sinking a ship is no way identify it."

"If it has good intentions, why choose that time to pass by without a flag?"

"It must be a navigation trial; when it lets itself go in the tempest the ship takes down its masts and sails, and is no longer anything but a box rolling on the waves—and at the right moment, the insect deploys its wings and antennae, and sails with perfect ease. The natives have also seen it, they say, floating in the air; perhaps it has a means of doing that."

"Indeed," said Roll. "It's convenient for going to the isles from which none return and planting its national flag there."

"If one could plant flags in the clouds, every aeronaut would do it."

One of the officers, who had raised the French flag over a group of islands south of the Isle of Pines stayed silent.

"At least possessions there cost nothing," said one of the scientists, naively, to break the slightly awkward silence.

The flow of the conversation was poor. Roll tried to redirect it by asking who had been manning the sunken launch. That reminded the governor of his guest's glories. "By convicts well known to you!" he said. "That was one of your triumphs—the Railway Bridge trial. Do you remember it?"

"No," said Roll, abruptly.

The governor, thinking that his guest's modesty needed to be swept aside, continued: "They featured in that mysterious affair, which you alone were able to clarify: the affair of the Railway Bridge remains one of your glories!"

Always that memory lashing him in the face! If Roll had been alone with the governor he would have made him pay for those words with his life.

While peeling a banana, the latter added: "Their names were Jacques and Jean Hénoe; the other one condemned in the trial, Pierre, is still at Île Nou, unless he's been killed by some accident last night. Those people didn't die after the sentences imposed for their first crime were commuted, and got away with it again after the fire in the prison—I think they've made a pact with luck."

That thought made Roll smile.

They did, indeed, have a pact with luck, good or bad—but the idea that his victims might once again be found in his path worried him. He experienced slight relief because two of the condemned had drowned, but the survivor irked him, as if he had slain a beast but a part of the beast refused to die. He reached the point of sensing them all around him; he was to become obsessed by that idea.

Anna also caused him some disquiet. His crime had been poorly buried while a single witness could rise up against him; that would have the effect of his brother's hands passing around his neck to threaten him.

Negligently, he replied: "What about the others, who perished with them?"

"Oh, the others were a Canaque and an eccentric convicted of blackmail—for political reasons, he said."

XIX. Not All Those Believed Dead Are

Josiah, although older, seemed more energetic still. If anyone had made a pact with Death it had to be him, for since the shipwreck in the Brest Channel he had sailed through tempests from one end of the Ocean to the other.

It is rare, when an individual escapes destruction, that a higher transformation does not take place within him. Nature herself, after every catastrophe, is subject to something similar. If Josiah, after his shipwreck, dreamed, as Olaff once had, about the fortunes of the world, it was not to hurl himself into futile adventures or to enrich a few rare companions, but to attempt the immense work of international justice.

The new world of which Olaff spoke tempted him like the shores of an unknown land. The form that transfiguration would take was a matter of indifference to him, as long as it happened. After one project, he would try another. With the stubbornness of a northerner, he was determined to live until the thing was begun.

In every individual, the same idea takes on a form appropriate to his particular organization, his character and his habit—his self, in sum.

Olaff had wanted to bring about the destruction of old laws by means of a universal uprising—but that revolutionary cyclone had probably gone to the bottom with the sunken millions of the *Whole*, a golden plan turned to dust, much to Josiah's regret.

Olaff, as a northerner, did not expect much of the human anthill. Was that because the masses had been unaware for myriads of centuries of the law of numbers, as wild beasts in menageries are unaware of the secret of their strength? A crack of the tamer's whip and a law whose crude bit tears the mouth a little more; that was sufficient to keep them down.

Before taking up the idea of a general uprising again, while letting the debacle of the centuries-long winter run to its completion, Josiah's plan was that of a navigator cradled by the Ocean. It was exactly the same project of which Julius had dreamed in Australia, as had the scientist Gaël, who had accomplished all his crimes and sacrifices for the sake of science, and was capable of killing the world and himself for a discovery, even if it only served to prolong the life of an insect.

Are not science, love and hatred rages: currents in which human microbes battle desperately, and which they sometimes contrive to master?

It was no longer an *idée fixe* that bore Josiah away but an *idée flottant*; it appeared to him everywhere like a phantom looming up in the midst of the terrible poetry of the Ocean.

Gaël had, or believed that he had, natural keys that opened the locks of secrets leading to the impossible, the magnetic currents of the globe, and those which, carrying away the human species, deny the elements of love. All that was known to him; he wanted to combine practice and theory, in a society with no other laws than those of the universe: a colony where nothing and no one would be tortured in order to obtain the deviations that cause our miseries and crimes.

Everyone follows his own attraction in his work, whatever his profession, toward some human group that will assimilate him and simultaneously spread his intelligence and that of others. Have you sensed, in great popular meetings, effluvia of ideas pass that are sometimes burning hot and sometimes icy? You live with the crowd; millions of lives are within you. The hatred, love and courage that carry you away are the very heart of the crowd, its intelligence—and its strength is multiplied infinitely. Then, by the light cast on the future, you see human groups gravitating in endless and boundless universal progress, as one sees with a telescope, beyond our rudimentary eyesight, stars rolling in the blackness of space.

Thus Gaël saw, incessantly solicited by the pressure of his brain, haunted by prodigious realities, which every century calls utopias but which, as they are attained, are the renewal of epochs.

Madame Basis still lived, and would live for a long time yet, since she expended so little intelligence, being accustomed to obey the doctor in everything. Her body was similarly slightly worn down, because she took a host of precautions that incessantly patched it up; thus, eternally preserved from everything that might destroy it, there was no reason why Madame Basis should not live for several hundred years. That was not her own desire, unless Gaël lived as long. Whatever she did, she only lived in order to watch over Gaël, in the continual dread that the doctor's diabolical thoughts and deeds might have both of them borne away by Satan.

The reason why Dr. Gaël had never thought of enabling Madame Basis to participate in the universal progress of beings by aiding her to emerge from her intellectual torpor is that scientists never pay any attention to what surrounds them, but only that which is far away.

Lafontaine's astronomer allowed himself to fall into a well while examining the distant stars.[24]

For a long time, Madame Basis hoped that Gaël would not leave Europe; she had eventually have understood the doctor's slowness in taking passage was because he had a cargo to assemble—seeds, microscopes, telescopes, pencils, paper, parchments, printing-presses and letter-stamps in all languages known or unknown, instruments of physics, surgery and music, alembics for distillation—and required specific certification from all the academies of Europe. On a scientific excursion, Dr. Gaël had an urgent need of all those things. No commander of a vessel wanted to load such a cargo for a single passenger, but an American ended up consenting, having his frigate followed by an old hulk patched up for the occasion at the expense of the academies, containing a part of what he called the doctor's "trinkets." The rest never quit Gaël; he slept on the deck of the *Margaret*, between his carefully-aimed telescope and a cup of herbal tea religiously brought by Madame Basis, which the doctor no less religiously knocked over when he got up to examine the stars.

"Since that devil of a man is always awake," said the mariners, giving a dab of the mop to the pool of tea, "he could easily go as far as the poop; that would be more appropriate." Gaël seemed to them to be some kind of old maniac, but they held him in higher consideration when, the captain of the *Margaret* and the sea-dogs, including the helmsman, having been poisoned by eating a fish that Gaël had declared to be dangerous, he took command of the ship, while caring for the officers. Gaël

---

[24] The fable in question is actually one of those attributed to Aesop.

had reckoned with the illness, which was suppose to be fatal, and with the ship, which he had brought safe and sound after three stormy days, to the first available port.

By the time he left the boat, Gaël had become a precious man. As for Madame Basis, there as elsewhere the good woman was regarded as an object always in a certain place. If she had not been there, something would have been missing, without anyone knowing what it was.

The trial colony had been founded several years before the epoch in which we find Josiah sailing the seas in his brig without a flag.

Treasures, weapons and wealth were amassed for the final battle, the battle of the desperate, which he anticipated. The Phantom Ship, as it was called in Noumea, picked up those wrenched from death and despair for the colony.

We know why the colony had been established in the northern wastes.[25]

Julius and his friends had hesitated between the unknown and free regions of Africa and those of the poles, but Gaël took the view that scientific missions were beginning to explore Africa; he knew scientists too well to trust them—and also, given that Africa has a generous climate, would it not be better to make a more decisive trial in a bitter ingrate nature, where necessity would compel invention?

---

[25] In fact, readers of *Les Microbes humains* would be surprised to find it there, having expected it to be established in Antarctica, and might not find the following explanation for the change of venue convincing. Presumably the awkwardness arises from the attempt to integrate what were originally two separate stories into one.

Thus, the poles were chosen. Having hesitated between the two, Josiah gave the advice that the riches known to him alone in the southern lands ought not to be risked, in the event that a superior force might come to destroy the nascent colony. With the treasures of the south they would either be able to found another colony, or facilitate what Olaff had attempted to do. Rumors of war haunting Europe caused him to anticipate the latter, but, on the other hand, peace might maintained between the nations, and perhaps their union under a single denomination: Europe, of which all the nations would be like provinces of the same fatherland. And there were so many other possibilities, full of the vision of the welfare of humankind, preceded by the terrible agony of everything that did not wish to die and the pangs of that which was seeking to be born.

XX. The Fugitives

When the four desperate men manning the launch had realized that the mass against which the tempest was driving them was not a reef but a ship, hope had given them a strength in proportion to the peril.

The lightning had shown them the brig, from which they must also have been seen; the hope was as great as the peril.

They heard, close at hand, the waves and wind attacking in the tempestuous night; the peril was greater, but salvation as at hand.

Half by instinct and half by virtue of having seen it in the previous cyclone, Jacques had recognized the Phantom Ship, the brig that passed by every three years in the tempest. His adventurous nature attracted him to the legend; the desire to solve the mystery gripped him, and gave his muscles the strength and suppleness that he needed.

More by intuition than anything else, for the violence of the sea and the wind drowned out the voices that were calling to them, the fugitives attempted the boarding. The waves carried them, and they arrived on the ship thrown on to the deck by the sea, which was rising furiously all the way to the bulwarks.

The brig was watching for them; the appearance of the launch was suggestive of an escape.

"Secure yourselves!" cried Josiah, in a thunderous voice; he had felt the human packages fall with the wave. Then, like a box, the brig was sealed, rolling with the tempest.

It was thus that the four escapers were saved by the peril itself, as their launch was engulfed.

The wreckage of the launch was found the following day, to Roll's great joy—a joy in which there was a lingering doubt, however, the sea being so perfidious that it might have left the importunate witnesses alive.

They were, indeed, alive, and they were already far away, sailing over the Ocean in Josiah's brig, through the abysms of the Ocean and the wrath of the wind. Josiah had never had such mastery of the elements; he played with them.

In the free groupings where new aptitudes developed, acquired knowledge was increasing. The idea stirred incessantly, forces were incessantly solicited; union, for great works or perils, in which all will and courage were united—all that could not be sterile.

The aptitudes newly developed had awakened others, to such an extent that an enormous ascensional movement was carrying all minds—and, in consequence, the entire colony—in a progressive direction.

Jacques was to find painters there with practiced and accurate eyes, and sure, broad hands, rendering the magnificent horrors of the ice and the beauties of the polar aurora. He heard choirs more beautiful, more terrible and sweeter than those he had been able to imagine, as great as those of cyclones, and as soft as the songs of breezes.

The wind and rain accompanied harps violins and basses, which had, like the voices, new notes at enormous distances, and an extreme delicacy likewise.

Jacques fell into ecstasy then, forgetting life in the acuity of the enjoyments of art.

There were few colonists as yet—only a few thousand—but scientific discoveries had progressed in the same way as the arts. For a long time, Gaël's telescopes and microscopes—all his scientific "trinkets"—had been accompanied by so many others that he spent entire days on the caverns where they were set up, nourishing his eyes, his heart, his intelligence and his entire being, for the inventions of human knowledge brought back from every voyage by Josiah served as a basis for new discoveries and inventions.

In the depths of its caves, under the ground, the colony was in advance of the science of Europe, and even over those that had not yet be adopted by the institutes; they would all have trembled if they had known about Gaël's next exploits—which, he said, would bring about the end of war.

XXI. In the Ice

In the region of Siberia that the Russian government has chosen as a place of deportation, the cold is terrible; it is the season of death—the black moon, as the Basques call it. Indeed, winter, enveloped by a shroud of snow, is a deadly night. The north wind blows for six months with the icy breath of the pole.

The summer, brief and hot, hastily exhales all the heat concentrated in the heart of the earth.

From time to time, one of the condemned lies down on the ground, exhausted, and no longer asks for his bread, but the repose from which one does not wake again. Others escape, gazing before them at liberty, as at a star.

There, as everywhere, the idea that will be the dawn shines in the great white plains, in the ice where the wolves prowl, as in the sunlit lands and beneath the oaks of Gaul. The men of the North, whose blood remains warm beneath the ice, dream there, in desolate wilderness of the Urals, as in the infernal mines of the Caucasus.

Josiah found it quite easy, from the nest that he had built, to set foot on that landing-ground, in order to join those who wanted egalitarian justice more than life and death. Among the exiles, there were people whose hearts nothing could stifle; the more solitude surrounded them, the more clearly the saw the deliverance that the anxious Earth awaits in its tortures.

Such were the two brothers Miralowski, seized by the current, or simply by the chance that determines so many things that many seem to have been organized, so neatly to their fall. Following their natural course, events, like everything else, have their harmony.

The idea of escape gripping them more powerfully one evening in the Siberian winter, the brothers set down the tools with which they were working on furs and, instead of going back to their beds, they sheathed their hunting knives, picked up their rifles, with powder and bullets, and parceled up their most indispensable clothing—two or three shirts of coarse fabric. The clothes that they were wearing ought to last a long time, being made of white furs—for, like the polar beasts, they could if the need arose be confused with the snow.

What had they to dread, Ivan and Fedor? Death by cold takes you like a dream, and death is eternal liberty. If they did not succumb, there would be a renewal of the struggle—which is to say, the incessant drive toward the end to be attained. Then again, they loved the unknown, the brothers Miralowski—who were twins, like the Wolff brothers, and, like them, similar in features, stature and nature; they were necessary to one another and sometimes, so common were their thoughts, they wondered whether they did not have the same breath of life, and whether one of them could have existed without the other. Both were tall, as red-haired as the aurochs, wild beasts with broad torsos; one might have thought them men of stone, so rude and monumental were they in their appearance; fundamentally, they were gentle and proud, terrible and merciful.

As with Roll and Philippe, it would not have been possible to tell Ivan and Fedor apart if they had not cut their red beards differently, Ivan's pointed, Fedor's crescent-shaped.

They had a good supply of powder and bullets, and a few pieces of dried meat. As for something to drinking, would not the snow and the ice give them that?

In the cold of that night, they drew away slowly, without speaking. Did they not understand one another?

The versts succeeded one another without their seeing anything but a black fox or the shadow of a wolf fleeing over the matt white of the snow. The silence, increasingly profound, gave their senses an intense acuity; the distant footfalls of a bear seemed to them to be close at hand, although it was on the horizon. Rare bushes raised their snow-covered branches above the limitless sheet, like apple-trees in May.

Finally, roofs appeared, like stains in the dull whiteness; they were the habitations of peasants, surrounding those of a gold-prospector. In the master's palace, the windows were shuttered; in the serfs' huts, the skylights were open.

The two brothers went into a wood-pile to wait for a favorable moment, when they could pass by without risk, for a road went through the village. The silence rendered them less circumspect, however, and they took the risk. Chance favored them; they went through without raising the alarm.

What point was there in resting in inhabited places? Would it not expose them to possible betrayal? The marched on for a long time. One of the branches of the Obi barred their route; once they had swum across, they would rest. We say "swum" because dislocated ice was floating with the current, held here and there by colder ice.

The night was followed, without any change in the landscape, by another day. At the steady pace of the bear, the brothers marched from their awakening until evening, only stopping for a few moments, standing up, leaning on their staffs—the repose of fugitives.

It was a matter of reaching the endless forests, where the partisans of Stenkorate[26] had once taken refuge, and where others arrived incessantly, in order not to pay their "father" the Tsar the tribute of conscription of taxation. There, in the profound woods, they lived side by side with the wolves; the bears visited their bees, but no human approached, fearful of not coming back.

You know Melly's verse:[27]

Oh, persuade the beasts, the advancing plague,
The winds, the blind lightning, the deaf sea.
But never ask anything of humans.

Humans do not go near the refugees living tranquilly since the time of Stenkorate, and the song of the old man is still on all lips, when limbs are attached to a gibbet above a fire of coals, and then whipped on the burns, the nails torn out and a saw passed through the flesh all the way to the bone, by order of the Tsar, the Voivodes and doubtless the priests—for they make treaty with the master's hand. For the defense of the muzjiks, Stenkorate—the bandit, the aristocrats call him; the dear father, say the poor—sang his death-song.

---

[26] This individual seems to be an invention of the author's; at any rate, I cannot find any trace of any such legendary figure.
[27] Possibly Charles Du Bois-Melly (1821-1905).

Bury me where three roads meet.
The roads to Kiel, to Saratov and Tula,[28]
Make of my bones a mound of earth,
At my feet, bury my sword, my terrible sword.
Those who pass by will salute liberty, and say
That the terrible Stenkorate is buried here,
Stenkorate, who was the defender of the barefoot!

They put him on the wheel in the presence of his brother Fiole; after his limbs had been torn off, the latter fell to his knees before the Tsar. "Shut up, dog!" cried the tortured man.

The legend of Stenkorate still floats over the Russian steppes of Europe and Asia. The people do not want him to be dead. The brave Stenkorate is beside the Volga, in a mine; they have seen him sitting motionless, thinking about the future of the people.

A little girl who was gone out to pick wild fruits saw Stenkorate lying on the ground with two eagles on his breast, tearing out his heart. Another saw him in a pond, with serpents and leeches sucking his bones, scorpions stinging him, toads drinking over him—such are the legends. Is not Stenkorate the Russian people torn apart by its masters?

Of the two eagles of the legend, the first has flown away; the second will take flight.

The legend of Stenkorate, and strange as that of Tell, accompanied the fugitives, soothing their monotonous march. Over the pathless steppes they went on and on, sensing that by the time their departure was noticed,

---

[28] The original has "Savtoff" and "Toula" here, "Sautoff" and "Toulo" when a variant verse is quoted subsequently, but the cities I have substituted seem the likeliest referents.

they would be so far away that no one would be keen to follow them through the cold, over the plains where wolves hunt, even if no one was fooled by the disorder, indicative of a catastrophe, that they left behind in their cabin—an old rifle lying on the ground, with Ivan's hat nearby, with the appearance of having been turned inside out by a bear.

The furry gentleman ought, in any case, to have visited them since their departure; they had left enough honey on the table and in the surroundings to tempt him, in spite of the distance. Some old growler ought to have left enough footprints in the snow to fool people, their own snowshoes having been put to backwards until they were some distance away. The simplest precautions succeed better than others; and then again, the falling snow covers tracks.

Once at the swollen river, which had to be the Obi, the two brothers consulted one another with their gaze. The only means of getting over it was to swim, as they had seen many others do. They were surprised, however, to see half a dozen well-armed men arriving at a fast pace, of a slightly theatrical warrior appearance. To flee would be to give themselves away, so the two brothers adopted the attitude most capable of inspiring the opinion that they were traveling in perfect security.

The man who seemed to be the leader of the troop approached the travelers. He was a young man with an insignificant but pleasantly symmetrical face and sympathetic eyes—a kind of human statue in wax.

"Well, comrades," he shouted, "Have you seen it?"

"Yes," Ivan replied, thinking that the affirmation would buy them time and that he would have an opportunity to discover what he had seen.

"Which way did it go?"

"To the other side of the river," Fedor added, thinking that it would be a means of crossing in a group, which would simplify the difficulty.

"It must have swum over, like a man."

The fugitives deduced that it was a matter of a bear.

"It went over on an ice-floe," Fedor replied.

"And how long have you been following it?"

"We were hunting it and lost sight of it. We've been searching for some time, but it was only a little while ago that it passed by."

"We need to get over the water. Are you with us?"

The two brothers nodded their head affirmatively.

"You live locally?"

"Yes, not far away in the woods. We were on our way home, following the bear."

"You're forest-dwellers?"

"Yes."

On the one hand, that affirmation cast a chill, for the inhabitants of the forests were reckoned to be savages, and the hunters seemed to belong to something akin to the colonial administration; on the other hand, the savages had a reputation for boundless bravery, and were useful companions.

"How do we get over?" the young hunter demanded.

It was an unnecessary question. The two brothers and one of the hunters accustomed to the rigors of the region had already set off on the perilous crossing, sometimes swimming and sometimes leaping from one ice-floe to another. The young man and the remainder of his retinue, not wishing to be backward in their boldness, launched after them.

The crossing which seemed impossible at first glance, presented few real dangers but numerous inconveniences—the cold of the water; the difficulty of reaching and steering ice-floes; fatigue. Eventually, first the two brothers and then all the others found themselves on the far side of the river

The bear must be far away, but he had had the pleasure of an exciting crossing, which was already something in the life of a governor's nephew; such was the rank of the young hunter, Alexis Ivanoff.

There was a fir-wood nearby; resinous branches made a magnificent fire, intended both to dry them and keep the wolves away.

One of the first barriers had been surmounted; still placidly, the two brothers stayed with their companions.

"The bear we're hunting has a history," said Alexis.

"Oh, we don't know anything in our woods."

"Well, this bear has devoured two men, among the strongest one can see, much like you: fellows that one might think made of granite. The cabin was ravaged; the brothers Miralowski must have been asleep; no one can understand how the animals were able to devour them without a struggle."

"Perhaps there were several bears," said Ivan.

"That's probable. Anyway, no one had seen one, but I promised my uncle, the governor of Tobolsk, to come back with the rascal's skin in time for the feast-day, which is in a week."

"If the bear doesn't have any particular mark, we might be in error. How big is it?"

"As big as a year-old colt."

"That's the one," said Ivan.

"Brown in color?"

"Absolutely!" Fedor agreed.

"It ought to have grey hair on its muzzle—it's an old one."

"There's no doubt!" said Alexis. "Now, you seem to me to be skillful hunters; we'd rather have that bear than two or three others—it's a matter of vengeance, you see. We don't do as much for deportees who are carried off by malady or misery, but when it's a bear, believe me, one avenges a man—and then again, when a bear has its legend, the man who kills it has a share in its glory."

"That's quite natural," said Ivan.

"Personally, I'd give Tobolsk for that bear. How about you, Vasili?"

"I'd throw in Siberia too, if I hadn't consigned it to the Devil."

As if to back up the fugitives, and enormous brown bear with a graying muzzle—a terrible old man of a bear—passed majestically by, rolling like a ship and dreaming beneath its thick fur.

Don't worry, friend Bear, thought the brothers Miralowski. *You've helped us on our way, and we'll leave you your life.*

The bear drew away at a mild trot, sensing that it was dealing with novice hunters and benevolent hunters; it sniffed such things in the air.

"You'll lead the hunt?" Alexis said to the two brothers.

"Gladly."

The hunters took a last drink from the gourds carried by Alexis and his companions. They were all eating, with the appetite of polar explorers, some sort of sun-dried reindeer meat. They got up from the fire, the two brothers guiding the hunt along a trail where they would not find the bear, but which brought the fugitives closer to the objective of their enterprise: to cross Siberia in the direction of the Bering Strait, and, as that part of North

America was no longer Russian since Alexander II, the Dynamited, had lost it in a card game, they would be free there.[29]

The Miralowski brothers' plan was to cover a good day's march in company with Alexis. Security at the beginning of a journey is a good way of putting one on the way to success.

With the most scrupulous attention, Ivan and Fedor took turns finding the tracks of the bear, explaining to the hunters a host of things at which they marveled. The hunt, carried away by youthful ardor, went over the steppes at a gallop. Just as they were about to catch up with the beast, it disappeared. Perhaps it was a mirage, perhaps it was a ruse employed by the bear to escape its enemies.

The best part of the affair was that the bear, as if it wanted to mock its pursuers, gravely retraced its steps and lay down beside the abandoned fire, cleaning its paws with particular care.

In the morning, Ivan and Fedor, incessantly deploring the hunt's bad luck, set out on campaign alone. They wanted to drive out the bear, and in spite of the opposition of the other hunters, they plunged into the woods—where, they said there were signs of the bear's presence. They never came back.

Doubtless the bear had eaten them. That increased the Alexis' ardor for vengeance, and he swore not to re-

---

[29] Tsar Alexander II preferred to be known as "the Liberator," because of his emancipation of the serfs. He sold Alaska to the U.S.A. for seven million dollars. He was assassinated by members of the Narodnya Volya [People's Will] organization in 1881, so this interpolated story must have been written after that date.

turn to Tobolsk without the skin of the bear that had devoured two men for a second time.

Poor Martin preferred a feast of honey, and, with a dignified self-possession worthy of eulogies for a hunted individual, it went forth, nicely warmed up, to procure one by overturning the beehives of the forest villages.

While Alexis sought to ignite his comrades' ardor with a speech, a courier who had been searching for them since the day before succeed in catching up with them, thanks to particularity of the Northern wastes that allows the sound of a voice to be heard several leagues away. Alexis' voice, high and very shrill, had reached him through the profound silence.

"Milord," he said, "The rumor's going around that the Miralowski brothers aren't dead; they've escaped in order to take a cargo of dynamite to Tobolsk. There's a price on their heads. You mustn't stay here, exposed to the danger of encountering those bandits. You might come to grief. Come back now."

Frightened, Alexis followed the courier, bitterly regretting the loss of the two brave hunters, who could have defended him so effectively against the Miralowski brothers.

The latter were still going on, between the Obi and the Yenisei, while the news of their escape and the promised reward filed the steppes with human packs hunting men—packs as unconscious as dogs or ferrets trained to pursue game.

The Miralowski brothers were unaware of that circumstance. It was at the moment when they were beginning to think they were safe that their situation was revealed in a terrible fashion.

In the profound forests that they had already glimpsed was salvation. They were crossing a plain half-filled with ruined huts around some kind of fortified house. It was the second habitation they had encountered in the space of thirty leagues; further on, they would be even more widely spaced.

That thirty leagues, traveled as of in a dream, made them think that they had a thousand to go, in even more difficult circumstances, before reaching the Bering Strait—but the forests were not very far away; there they would find friends.

The Miralowski brothers did not torment themselves mentally; they knew what they had to do; having begun the enterprise, they went forward without useless regrets or puerile fears.

This time, a real danger presented itself. In the village they had encountered, overlooked by the fortified house, they observed a movement similar to the agitation of ants. It was, in effect, a human ant-hive in motion. There was a working mine there, and its owner was living there, according to the custom of the Siberian plains, until he had made enough money to leave. As for the wretched workers gathered around him, let them do what they liked; were they not free to stay there or dig elsewhere? Usually, they stay.

The latter were swarming in the mine and the surrounding area in the greatest activity, to bring forth riches that not one of them would touch, less intelligent than the ants and bees who work for their whole society without anyone in the hive dying of starvation. Insects are not stupid enough to be unaware that everyone's life is dependent on everyone else's.

A courier at the door of the house, standing up in his stirrups, read from the height of his grandeur—rather than that of his little horse with bristling hair—a proclamation of His Majesty the Tsar, our father, which enjoined everyone to search with the utmost diligence for the two fugitives, who must be at the head of a formidable conspiracy. A hundred roubles a head was offered for the arrest of the two brothers.

The master of the mine had summoned all his muzjiks to hear the promise. Did they not share in the tsar's danger, since the tsar is the people? Like the legend of Stenkorate, he is the poor people devoured by eagles and bitten by serpents.

All the unconscious townspeople, some having come up from the mine and others out of huts, gathered around the courier. At the same time as the two brothers came in view of the inhabitants of the town, the courier came within theirs.

There was no room for doubt; they were the fugitives.

The entire human pack surged toward Ivan and Fedor; they hardly had time to place themselves back-to-back in order to cover all sides, and draw their knives.

A savage battle began: a battle of wild beasts, in which teeth and claws are more terrible than steel. Cornered like wild boar, they held out for an hour; the earth around them was red.

"We'll have to share the roubles," said the master of the mine, Boris Volke, to the courier, Vasili, while the assailants, like members of a dog-pack, rolled down the slope and surged back up even more furiously to attack the fugitives. They both laughed, one from the back of his horse, the other in his big fur boots.

"Bravo, Gessoff! Bravo! He's got an ear, the brave Givotnoye!"

"Bold Agnenoke! Good for you, Black Staroui!"

The courier laughed wholeheartedly.

One after the other, the two brothers fell, striking the air with their massive arms. A muzjik wilier than the rest had deprived the two brothers of their foundation; the fellow had slipped the barrel of a rifle through the mob and out bullets in their legs. It was the loss of blood rather than the pain of the bullets lodged in their flesh that exhausted them.

Lifting them up by the shoulders and the feet the muzjiks brought back their double prey, completely inanimate. A deathly pallor covered the faces of the two brothers; the blood was still flowing, making a red pool at their feet.

Laid on the ground, it seemed that they would never regain consciousness.

Hungry for the reward, thirsty for blood, rendered more furious by the wounds they had received, the entire pack surrounded Volke and the courier. There was no fear that the dead men, laid down on the master's pavement, might get up again. The reward was disputed with such howls and groans that Volke, amused by it, strung out the scene.

"Hey, Master Courier, you haven't got off your horse, although the thing's already done. Get down—we have time now; you can rest a while and take tea. And you, dogs, back to the kennels! The spoils will be distributed later."

But the arguments that had flared up were not finished; everyone, no longer aware of anything but his avidity for battle, was fighting, more entertainingly than cocks or bulls. Boris and the courier were taking an equal pleasure in it—so much so that they did not hear the door of the room in which the wounded men had been placed closing softly.

XXII. Marpha Wolke

It was a young woman with light brown hair and steel-blue eyes, proud and sometimes implacable, as tall and thin as a fir-tree, who had closed the door. She tapped one of the paving-stones with her foot, which was lifted up a moment later. A young man, closely resembling the woman who had summoned him so strangely, having the same audacious face beneath the red pelt of the North, emerged from the trap-door, at which a spiral staircase terminated.

"Mikhail, these are the fugitives they're going to give to the tsar."

"Are they dead?"

"I don't know. Get them down, quickly!"

In response to his companion's orders, the other summoned more men. The two bodies were taken down, with all possible speed and precaution; then the trap-door closed again.

Marpha left the room. She was just in time; her father came back in with the courier and the muzjiks who worked in the kitchen.

Nothing had been disturbed in the room from which the bodies had vanished.

In one of the neighboring rooms, Marpha could be heard singing, accompanying herself on the piano, the song of Stenkorate:

Bury me far away in the plain,
Where the three roads meet.
In the ebony veil of night,
My hands will emerge from the earth.

In the shadows they will show you
The way to Tula, Saratov and Kiel.
At my feet beneath the somber earth,
Place my sword, still stained with red.

As somber as the legend, Marpha's voice rumbled with menace; that of her cousin, Mikhail Volke, replied from afar with the final verse:

Those will possess the earth
Who have the number and the equity.
I shall return for the great war,
The great war for liberty!

Marpha understood from her cousin's tone, and from the meaning of the verse, that the fugitives were not dead.

The scene unfolding in the other room was of very different in kind.

The disappearance of the two bodies filled Volke, the courier and the muzjiks with anger and dread. The wretches had pretended to be dead and had made off with the bullets in their legs. Now these accursed birds of revolt could fly with lead in their wings. What was our father the tsar going to say?

It was just at the moment when a conspiracy had been discovered.

"And what about the reward! It's Agenoke's fault—he said they were dead."

"No, it's Black Staroui's!"

"It's Gosssoff's!"

"No, it's Givotnoye's!"

They accused one another so fiercely, hunting dogs giving voice, howling and growling, that three of them— Gossoff, Staroui and Givotnoye—were accused of facilitating the prisoners' escape.

All things considered, they could not get far in that state; it was only necessary to search the vicinity to recapture them; the plain on the far side of the mine extended as smoothly as a mirror, with not a wrinkle in the ground.

What motive for the muzjiks have had for opening the door? It was in their interest for the prisoners to remain in the hands of the man who promised a reward; if some of them were in accord with the fugitives, that was a serious matter!

In the meantime, those accused by the others would be put in a cell and the courier would carry away the news.

"Marpha! Marpha!" cried the three wretches, with the result the young woman came out of her room to see who was calling her.

"What do you want?" she asked.

"You know full well, dear Marpha, that we're not guilty."

"Guilty of what?"

"Of having saved the two strangers—on the contrary, we wanted to hand them over."

Fear caused them to forget Marpha's character.

"Is that really true?" she asked. "You wanted to hand them over?"

"Yes—we're the ones who caught them."

"And you're asking me for mercy?"

"Yes, dear Marpha. Plead for me."

Volke, who adored his daughter, softened his heart; at her request, he was ready to grant mercy, without worrying about the tsar—but she looked into the faces of the wretches whose hands were clasped with her savage eyes, and enveloped her father with the same gaze.

"No!" she said. "I won't beg for mercy for dogs who hand over their brothers." And she turned around, grimly, leaving her father and the three muzjiks stunned.

That woman's part of the conspiracy, thought the messenger.

She was, in fact, part of a conspiracy—but not the one he thought.

XXIII. The Red Wedding

Volke adored his daughter, but that was not is only affection; he had almost as much for his nephew Mikhail, whom he had brought up.

Mikhail was the son of a brother whom he had lost. Born on the same day, and never having been parted, the two children were cast into such despair that they had ended up being allowed to stay together. They had also made their studies together; gripped by the same currents, they were now affiliated to the nihilist party.

It was the revolution that they loved in them, with a boundless love, knowing full well, by virtue of the reprisals the tsar inflicted on those who fell into his hands, what fate awaited them; they not only demanded to live together, but to die together.

There are red weddings, in which Death seals the vows; they are the most beautiful; they are never broken. Thus Marpha and Mikhail were espoused, one day in bright sunlight, in the imperial square of Tobolsk.

This is what happened. Marpha and Mikhail, whose studies had been fruitful, were skillful doctors; once the bullets were extracted from Fedor's and Ivan's wounds, they had healed rapidly.

Hidden in the cellars, one of whose secrets exits we have seen and which had been hollowed out by their collaborators, the fugitives, once fit again, having enough roubles to facilitate their journey, dressed in clothes as solid as their own but different in form, were able to go on without being troubled. Marpha had given them specimens of minerals, which are numerous in the plains of Siberia. The rich exploiters who raised their palace-like tents would open their way. Was that not sufficient for them to reach the forests where the sons of Stenkorate's partisans had built their townships?

Mikhail and Marpha, having embraced the Miralowski brothers, let them go. With the aid of the villages in the forests, they reached the Bering Strait, having given the slip many times to those who were searching for them, whose instincts of avidity they had aroused thanks to their mineral specimens, mocking the tsar and his minions.

They might have been caught there, having covered eleven hundred leagues successfully, were it not for the commander of a brig, who declared that they were his passengers, whom he had sent out in search of various minerals. The sight of the specimens, which Josiah claimed that he would soon hand over for the exploitation of Russian capitalists, and the assurances he gave them that certain stones in their quarries also contained gold, dazzled their eyes so well that he was able to add the two Russians to those he had collected throughout the world for the polar colony.

On the same day that Josiah took them aboard his brig, the streets of Tobolsk were flooded; they were hanging two nihilists accused of plotting an attempt on the tsar's life.

That was the result of the courier's denunciation. An infamous plot had been discovered, for, in searching beneath the paving-stones, a clandestine printing-press had been discovered, like one that had been found in Moscow. The two affairs had been combined under the usual heading: conspiracy again the tsar.

In order to imprint the terror of repression more fully on the masses, the two nihilists from Moscow and the two in the jurisdiction of Tobolsk were each executed in the capital of the province where their crime had been committed.

Neither city was terrified; the nihilists had no fear of death.

The unconscious part of the population believed that it would be saved from a danger by the disappearance of a few individuals; as for the conscious part, even knowing how many enemies it had, tortures suffered for a cause rendered it all the dearer.

The best means of increasing a revolt is to do everything one can to destroy it, as those who die for liberty do not regret life.

Before the executioner put the sacks over their heads to hide the faces of those o be hanged, Mikhail and Marpha looked at one another, smiling—and that as all.

The first to be taken up was Marpha. Mikhail saw her body fall into empty space. Then it was his turn. He went up rapidly, in haste no longer to be, she being no more.

During the night, the nihilists placed re crowns under the scaffold. Was it not Mikhail and Marpha's wedding—the red wedding?

A new recruit joined the revolution. Boris Volke swore to avenge his children. It would not be out of conviction but out of love for his beloved dead that he would fight, but the result would be the same.

XXIV. Liberty

The pink granite port of Sydney opens against a horizon of blue mountains with less grandeur than the port of the free colony against the ice of the pole.

The town is partly sheltered by the sheer wall of rock that protects a chain of volcanic mountains crumbled into caverns, and partly surrounded by a branch of the Gulf Stream that flows around it in order rediscover the current, which it rejoins beneath the waves.

That peninsula, a veritable oasis, had been discovered by Josiah.

There are two towns, one in the open air for the brief summer, the other underground in the caves, for the long polar winter; there are located the forges, the alembics and the retorts of the laboratory, which is also the arsenal, in which the refugees are preparing, for the battle of the weak against the strong, weapons capable of destroying the world—and which, in consequence, will render all war impossible.

With the means furnished by science and by the instinct that develops the faculties of humans and other living beings, in accordance with the environment, almost everywhere, they were able to live there, and to sustain their collective struggle against nature and against the death that would have claimed them if they had ceased.

That only made them stronger.

The atmosphere of that magnificent perpetual struggle of individuals united in peace against nature in fury had the same effect on those individuals as the emanations that gorged the vegetables of buried epochs and made them giants. In that human hive, all the bees made honey, and the idea never occurred to anyone of refusing it to those who absorbed more or of seeking to store it for their own use. Why do that? Did not everyone have enough for their own needs?

The vain objections of those who apply to the life of tomorrow the mores of today are worthless. The new era will not feature the rags of today any more than it will sound our alarm bells. No one can fall into abysses that no longer exist.

Everyone donated their intelligence, their strength, their heart, consuming what was necessary to their physical and intellectual existence. In that respect, Gaël was a veritable alembic; his brain ground up and devoured everything that the inventors of Europe were scarcely beginning to glimpse; he took the poor little seeds of our sciences in order grow marvelous sheaves therefrom. The colonists came together voluntarily, as the birds flock together to fly through the air and wild cattle herd together to stand off wolves. Since languages were also evolving there, so was human anthropology, in all its forms; nothing remained the same.

Thus, in an enormous increase on the fertile soil, free men will come together on the free earth after the deliverance.

Like heavenly bodies gravitating in space, humans and societies will organize, for the conscious and voluntary labor that will bring forth abundant crops where there were fallow fields, happy societies where there were miserable ones, as in the colony in the ice, but with the difference between a city and an entire world. The force of tempests and gulfs will break upon the rocks, will open passes through mountains, one more implement in the service of humankind.

Submarine vessels exploring the sea-beds will discover buried continents; the cyclopean ruins of Atlantis will reappear to us beneath their watery shroud, beneath the corals and the seaweed—Atlantis, and perhaps other lands.

Electricity will bear airships over the polar ice beneath the red fringes of the polar auroras.

How many things will be discovered when we look forward, forgetful of our wretched individuality? Personalities will be very different when everyone lives in humankind entire, infinitely multiplying its strength, its thought, its existence.

The ideas of liberty and justice, so long advertised on the human prisons in which nascent ardent desires have been confined, will display in their true light the things that obscurity makes vague and deceptive. They will grow incessantly, those ideas of egalitarian justice, stirred and fertilized by every thought.

You have seen the laborers turning over the furrows in order to sow the new wheat; thus will the old crop of social iniquities be turned over and buried.

What is the good of the meanings of the arts, what is the good of the intelligence within us, it is stifled, in order to leave its benefits only to those who have neither arms not brains, but are only stomachs, like larvae? In those who live in leisure, the brain no longer receives the perception of the furrow beneath the plough; in those who labor and suffer too much, the brain is uncultivated, and ramifies at hazard.

Is not the powerful vegetation of virgin forests worth more than the bastardized culture of dwarf trees in Japanese vases; they must die quickly. Wait for the millennium to give way to the twentieth century, disencumbered of our follies, our stupidities and our miseries.

Every character and ever intelligence taking its place in the universal gravitation, having moved the earth to the benefit of all, the race will be so very different from the human cattle that you could turn every living human individual into the entire human species and the whole living human species into every individual, the idea moving forward in the great peace, so far that the horizon will be broader and broader as knowledge and intelligence grow.

That dream is, like all the hypotheses of an epoch, the reality of the one that follows.

Though myriads of cannons are aimed at the multitudes who rise up, that will not prevent it coming to pass, tomorrow or in a thousand years, because neither the human flocks nor the idea can die, and because the flocks will be humankind and the idea is the future; as for war, it is, except in the case of an idea, butchery, which will no longer be able to exist.

Large drops fall before a rainstorm, and suddenly, they pour in torrents on the desiccated earth. The space where the desperate had taken refuge was to the denouement what the large raindrops are to the storm they precede. They have had it up to the neck with everything they have seen or heard, driven by the fatality of our order of things, and they want no more of it. That is why they must either die or life for the future. They are living for the future.

XXV. The Banque de Fumosas

Do you know the gold mines that provide the capital of the famous Banque de Fumosas? No, you don't.

It had a brief vogue; there are thousands like that, whose capital is situated in the sea-mists, carrying off, by way of ballast, the money of fools. So much the better, after all—it assists the bankruptcy of human stupidity.

The founder of the bank was a ferret-faced dwarf as fat as a balloon, who claimed to be the owner of mines in the Spanish colonies in which the sand and rocks were full of gold nuggets. There might well have been gold in the rocks, but he did not possess a single one in daylight. What he possessed was the art of fishing for fools, with hooks that are more reliable when the deception is cruder. I believe that people like being defrauded.

The dwarf had such a cynical fashion of making mock of the world that he attracted considerable deposits. The business went admirably, for him, so long as people were content with promises, and there was nothing to prevent that lasting for as long as he needed to leave the country.

Christiano Del Mar had veritable genius: the genius of deception. No one had caught him out, and he expected to get away with in indefinitely. The dwarf was a specialist, claptrap bringing in a fat profit being the only string to his bow, he knew it inside out. With that string, he would vary tunes and play the notes that filled his wallet eternally.

The reputation of the Banque de Fumosas not only attracted fools but a worthy rival to Christiano Del Mar, the Greek Hymetta, whose name was as sweet as that of the beloved mountain of bees. Live everyone else, thieves only find salvation in audacity.

In fact, Hymetta was by no means of Greek origin, but being unable to reveal his civil status, having escaped from various places, he had procured Greek papers. The most recent escape was from Noumea, in an ecclesiastical costume, on a feast day. Embarking on a mail-boat, he had encountered and English clergyman; the two augurs looked at one another, laughing, and understood one another so well that the Englishman piloted the Frenchman, giving him letters of recommendation for a Russian businessman, and our man, passing himself off as a political exile, was entrusted to take his employer's savings and daughter to London.

By the time the latter perceived the theft perpetrated upon her father she already had a little girl; the Russian woman being proud, she died of shame.

Hymetta soon found that his frauds had been discovered and, no longer being able to stay in London, he placed his daughter, paying a thousand francs in advance for ten years, and came to Paris, where he lived for several years. Like Christiano Del Mar, Hymetta had a specialty, dealing in blackmail—a branch of the industry in which Del Mar had not yet dabbled.

The idea of a possible association between the two businesses occurred to Hymetta, who divined the kind of bank that the dwarf was running; he went to its offices, and the two odd fellows examined one another, Del Mar with his greenish eyes, supporting his chin on his hollow breast, Hymetta with his small black raptorial eyes. Each one was wondering how he could cheat the other, and also feeling a slight anxiety that he had seen someone vaguely similar to the other before.

After the conventional remarks about honesty, which rogues never fail to proclaim, the conversation took a different turn: the issuing of shares of the Banque de Fumosas, the returns that the shares would bring into the enterprise, and other matters in which the manipulators of other people's money deal with one another so easily.

The two men examined one another all the way to the entrails.

"It's strange," said Hymetta, finally, "how closely you resemble one of my old friends."

"What was his name?"

"Bosco—a name that had come from a roundness of the back that ran in the family."

"Which proves that wives are faithful."

"Indeed!"

The conversation languished momentarily; then Del Mar came to a decision and said: "For your part, you resemble one of my best friends so closely that I must ask you whether he's related to you; his name is Frérot—that's what his friends call him."

They had both recognized one another.

An association ensued—a formidable association, although it only had two members—which created a rain of money. They did not restrict themselves to vulgar frauds; there were terrible blackmails, for which they were never denounced because their victims did not want the shamed or misfortunes that the wretches had discovered to be publicized.

They examined the *Gazette des Tribunaux* minutely in search of what the law had not discovered. They succeeded well enough to become more audacious. The affair of the Railway Bridge came to their attention, and in the moments of respite given to them by the increasing prosperity of their cash-flow, they sought so assiduously that a part of the mystery appeared to them; in order to seek further enlightenment they looked for a few other trials connected with the affair, several cases often forming a whole.

The episode of Anna accusing Roll before the tribunal put them on the right track. It was only a matter of finding her or the children, to obtain proofs and to be paid a fortune for their silence.

The little ones having been put in a foundling home seven or eight years previously they must now be twelve or thirteen; it was possible to pick up their trail. Hymetta passed himself off as the unfortunates' uncle, declaring, in order to allay suspicion, that Anna was completely mad. He wanted to adopt his nephews; it was necessary that a search be carried out for them.

It was by crows that Roll was to be discovered.

The children were in the parlor when "Uncle Hymetta" came into the penitentiary colony, the person who had come to visit them being their old companion, now a locksmith, who brought "his children," as he called them, a few treats, for their live was hard and their privations constant. The arrival of the uncle did not cause André any excessive joy; he looked distinctly shady, and his vulturine appearance caused the young man to make the resolution to be more vigilant than ever.

Uncle Hymetta had no difficulty taking the two children away; he was their relative, and he flattened out the only difficulty. The children had been fed when they could not yet do very much, and now that they were working it was necessary to let them go—such was the hindrance that Hymetta knew how to overcome, with a tidy sum, which the two associates invested in the enterprise, sure that they would obtain a hundredfold return.

His children had often been hungry and cold, and had often been beaten, but never, since the time of the Red Room, had they been as frightened as they were by Uncle Hymetta, who reduced them to the state of a rabbit taken by force from its cage in order to be killed.

André was unable to obtain the uncle's address.

I can't do otherwise, he thought. He went out and waited, in order to follow Hymetta, who took the children away, the business not having taking long.

The administration was completely deceived, but André was not; that uncle frightened him.

XXVI. Who's Watching the Nest?
No one. Poor Little Birds

Fortunately for André, the road that took the children to Paris was difficult for horses. He followed the fiacre easily enough—but the opposite slope only permitted him to use the means that street-urchins use to get a ride; he leapt on to the back of the vehicle and clung on, risking his life at every moment, for Hymetta was in a hurry and the horse was now moving rapidly.

It stopped in front of the famous Banque de Fumosas. There the coachman threw his gray coat into the carriage, and seemed as well-dressed as Uncle Hymetta.

That precaution displeased André. Through the gilded gates of the courtyard he watched the lugubrious entry of the children, fluttering in bewilderment, like little birds fallen from the nest.

The two associates saw André' anxious face and, recognizing the young man, had a vague pang of anxiety. He had followed them, therefore he was an enemy, certainly an inconvenient observer.

Does a lion-hunter want to be anxious as to the fate of the kid tethered to the trap?

André disappeared, fearing that the children's situation had not changed. He scented a mystery. They had seen him too, and smiled at him from afar. It reassured them to know that André was watching over them.

"Who is that man?" Hymetta asked the children, as he took them into the house.

"It's André."

"Who's André."

"He's the one who looked after us when we were put in the colony."

André might be useful, and if he was not, he could easily be dealt with—such was the thought that occurred to the two associates simultaneously.

Hymetta and Del Mar made sure that the children confided to them were watched by their housekeeper, an old lady with a viperfish face who had also carried out an exchange of names and residences successfully: the widow Eleazer. She it was who would collect their slightest words and quickly clarify the matter. The widow had experienced the same attraction as the other two when they had encountered one another.

When that woman appeared before the children she frightened them more than Uncle Hymetta—but Andre knew where they were, they thought.

Yes, he knew that, as one knows what lies behind the walls of fortresses, without having the golden key that opens all doors.

The children had had a meager lunch in the colony, but hunger passed them by in confrontation with Uncle Hymetta and the housekeeper. They went to bed without speaking, not daring to communicate their thoughts to one another.

How can those who have lived for such a long time the life of a beaten animal, resigned and mute, expect anything good? Ill-treatment did not frighten them as much as other children; they were used to it.

There is nothing as sad as children like that, already aged by the habitude of bad days.

Charlot and Loulou were still small; poverty inhibits growth.

When they talked to one another, it was always about the past, their early childhood, the time when they were happy; that made them resemble old men, who remember the events of their youth better than those of recent times, and find the past better than the present— but isn't it always the same; and how can it change when the same past iniquities endure in our mores, so long as the raft of the *Medusa* cannot reach land?

Uncle Hymetta came to interrogate his wards.

"Let's see—you, the bigger one, what do you know?"

"I don't know."

"What did you do at the colony?"

"We carded wool in the winter; in summer, we went to get grass for the rabbits."

"Did you like that—the rabbits?"

"I don't know."

"Who ate them?"

"I don't know."

"And you—do you know?"

"No, I don't know either."

"Can you read?"

"I learned a little from Mama, and I taught my brother."

"Ah! You remember your mother?"

Always having been punished when they talked about their mother, they fell silent, thinking that it was a trap, and went pale.

For several days it was impossible to get them to talk. The two associates then had the bright idea of taking them to the house of the judge that Anna had accused of having murdered their father.

Judge Wolff had not been a judge for a long time; he had left at the head of the scientific mission that he had directed so well—but the house had not changed its appearance; from the exterior one could still see the same heavy and warm red curtains at the windows of the Red Room. That had been the nest of the judge's children.

XVII. The Ordinary End of an Insurgent

A revolutionary dies to the great delight of his enemies, who imagine that at least they have one fewer soldier to fight—but the army is now too numerous, the idea too clear, for a single drop of water to count in all the waves that are battering the breach of the old world.

It was neither decrepitude nor disease that had killed Marcel; he was strong and not yet old. Marcel was dead because his most ardent desire was about to be accomplished, because the red dawn of the new world was about to succeed the night and anyone would be able to see what he had dreamed of all his life.

Why? There are unconscious fatalities that strike nevertheless. Have you ever seen one of those men who can only become happy in order to fall more terribly? I'm not talking about the idiotic happiness of wealth, or what are called honors, but of something that is truly a joy, an immense joy capable of making the heart burst. One does not have those joys for long; one goes on until the moment when one has them, and then everything crumbles.

That is why Marcel was dead.

There was a red flag on the coffin followed by the procession of the poor.

It was a January morning heavy with snow; the red and black banners were flapping in the wind, which was blowing tempestuously.

No one was sad, though; why should they be? There had been no joy or sadness for a long time; a warm breath passed over the crowd, through death, through winter. There had been pressure, and an order not to raise the banners, but they had held firm and resisted.

The procession was numerous, some being there because the man who had died had carried the flag proudly, others out of curiosity; these curiosities often take hold, and once seized by them, one remains gripped.

At the windows, a few beautiful ladies hid themselves in order to watch; it is bad form to watch red flags pass by. There was more than one, however, whose heart was made to beat a little faster by the banner of revolt, women being natural insurgents.

Street-urchins hovered around the edges, not daring either to throw stones or shout as they were accustomed to do at the exits of meetings.

The people who pay instead of acting had once sent those bands of innocents against him, howling like a pack of animals, somewhat akin to the fireworks that are exploded by the sides of a bull in the arena: a spectacle all the more amusing because the man could not throw himself upon the children like a dog upon a flock; it was necessary to suppress his anger.

Marcel was liberated from such petty infamies, as from greater ones.

All these things had not troubled him unduly during his life, but in his brief death-throes he had shaken them off gladly, as one shakes off ordure fallen on one's clothes. How small a place the miseries of each individual occupy by comparison with the immensity of misery! Only one still seemed large to him—that was when his mother had been condemned to die when he had been sent to prison for a long time. And then, at the grave, his pardon had been thrown in his face.

It seemed to him that, in dying, he was ridding himself of all the memories of that cold cruelty, which he was about to forget in the dreamless sleep—along with other things—and then again, Marcel loved to analyze; it appeared to him to be good to taste death. Of the fruits of the tree of knowledge there was hardly any except that one he did not know, and it was perhaps the best.

Marcel had lived centuries in the short time separating his trial from his death; he knew that nothing can hold back the growth of peoples and that the humanity of his virile era would not resume the swaddling-clothes and gurglings of its cradle; thus, he died joyfully, hearing in the distance the stages of humankind's march. His trial was strange in its nature; impatient for better days he had wanted to hasten them, hasten them as much as possible, so he had acted in desperation.

If the story of that attempt were told, this book would not have appeared, although it is of the order of things that anyone can accomplish. And yet, whether its story is told or not does not make anything more or less than it is. When Germinal blows, some sing and others make the epic; all breathe it. Sometimes, Germinal has hasty flowers; such had been the goal of Marcel's attempt.

Judged and condemned to death, without wanting to put in an appeal for mercy, Marcel lived in the future more than ever; he went on and on, until the point where his mind became lost. The end of his life was in harmony with the rest; it was just, and that was what was astonishing.

He was right; the scaffold did not serve him as a podium to hurl the cry of universal deliverance into the crowd. At the podium he had forgotten the life of today for that of tomorrow. The new sun had inundated him;

he had been warm; he was cold on returning to his prison; that was simple, and it happens to everyone. His breast froze, and the thing went swiftly.

It would have been stupid for a man condemned to death to complain about feeling ill. Marcel went to bed as usual, but one day, he did not get up again. As usual, that death was attributed to something that had nothing to do with it. And, also as usual, although Marcel had not asked for any, mercy was granted. His body was therefore given to his companions in the struggle without any argument.

When the funeral cortege arrived at the gate of the cemetery of X***, large black clouds that had been threatening since the morning split, whipped by the wind. Thick snow decorated the red and black banners, like trees in May.

He had finished the voyage of life, in which so many shipwreck-victims devour one another. He had ended the somber voyage gazing at the harbor.

XXVIII. Blackmail

While alive, Marcel had been slandered by all sorts of people.

The venomous teeth of human rats are subject to such rages, without anyone knowing why. Perhaps it was because he did not bother to respond. Once dead, he would maintain silence even better, which was encouraging. Hymetta and Del Mars, tempted by that windfall, set to work in that direction too. You know the supposedly-proverbial saying: "Give me two lines of a man's handwriting and I'll guarantee to get him hanged."

There was no lack, not merely of lines but of pages of Marcel's handwriting. The dwarf, who imitated handwriting with an ape-like skill, fabricated a collection of letters to which even the postmarks gave an impression of authenticity.

Furnished with this work, Hymetta and Del Mar went to the offices of *La Débâcle*, a newspaper for which Marcel had written, and asked to speak to the editor about an important matter.

The two shady individuals, moving craftily and looking askance, reeked of treason from a mile away. Having sat down on the edges of their chairs and looked at one another for support, Del Mar commenced: "You've suffered a great loss."

The editor of *La Débâcle*, Albert Noret, a former friend of Julius Borelli, had a similar lack of confidence in people who were too polite and too unctuous. "Yes," he replied, dryly.

"It's in that regard that we've come to renew your dolor."

"I don't like beating around the bush; let's get to the point. Marcel owed you money and you've come to ask us to pay his debt."

"If it were only that!"

"Get on with it."

"Well, there was talk yesterday, in a circle where my associate and I were present, of letters compromising for your friend's honor."

"Marcel was incapable of any dishonorable action."

"You think so?"

"I'm sure of it."

"We have the proof," said Hymetta.

"What proof?"

Hymetta went on: "As Marcel's reputation belongs to a party, of which you're a member, and of which my associate and I are similarly..." He stopped.

"Get to the point."

"Well, we thought we ought to purchase a few of your friend's letters—the ones that might be abused."

"You've been deceived, Messieurs. Explain yourselves."

The rogues had no fear; they had circulated their fake letters via other hands and had ostensibly bought them. They were covered."

His back bent, Hymetta looked at the dwarf, who was padded on both sides in order to generalize his deformity, and who resembled a small barrel with two knock-kneed legs underneath; there is a symbol in the Egyptian alphabet that is absolutely similar.

These two beings, so different from one another, had one point of contact; if one were to touch their skin, one would have found it as cold as that of a reptile. The manner of intelligence was also in harmony.

"Show me these papers," said Albert.

"*These* papers, my dear Monsieur..." Looking up at Albert in the same way that a ferret looks at a bird, however, he saw that it was necessary to be wary.

The associates thought, too late, that it might be a trap for foxes rather than for rabbits; they were the ones in the net; they had acted like imbeciles. True, some years after Marcel's death they would not have found a buyer for the fake letters, but it was too soon; they had not studied the mores of the dead man sufficiently, and those of the friend to whom they were addressing themselves, the dead being less dangerous than the living.

What diabolical idea had they had? They could have earned more producing forgeries for autograph-collectors without any consequences. If they had not said that they had the letters on them, they could have replied without disaster.

Del Mar presented one of the letters.

The postmark had been counterfeited in accordance with a letter of the same day and year, addressed to a person who no longer existed; there were fewer risks that way.

They were in an awkward situation.

There was not much to be said against the envelope; then it fell apart. One could still read:

To Monsieur Philibert, Financier
96 Rue de Rivoli

My dear Philibert,
I have just completed a speculation that has made a hundred per cent profit. I offer you half of another of the same sort to be undertaken imminently.
Your humble servant,

MARCEL

Marcel, so proud, declaring himself the servant of the famous financier Philibert! It was a monstrosity.

Albert, thrown into a stupor by the perfectly-imitated envelope, was reassured as soon as he read the first words of the letter.

"How much did you pay for this collection?"

"A hundred thousand francs."

"That's too dear for us—but come back tomorrow at the same time." While speaking, he had copied the envelope, which he handed back to Del Mar.

The two associates, although anxious about that copy, could not refuse it; that would have given themselves away.

They took their leave of Albert and went out, very perplexed.

The next day, they read in *La Débâcle*:

Some wretches have sold Messieurs Del Mar and Hymetta a collection of fake letters, which they attributed to our friend Marcel, without even worrying about whether the edifice would crumble at the removal of the first stone.

Messieurs Del Mar and Hymetta, who have bought the collection for a hundred thousand francs and have just made us an offer to destroy it—on reimbursement of their funds, of course—will doubtless want to pursue this blackmail, whose authors they can identify.

This is a copy of one of the letters, dated Paris, 18 June 18 , a time at which we were both English prisoners of war in southern Africa. We had taken the side of the Zulus, who were fighting their war of independence. We were about to be shot, but a learned English general claimed that we had done some useful work, and they contented themselves with sending us to the Cape in company with Cetewayo, the Zulu chief.

You know what happened in the English colonies. The first, under the orders of Pearson, was blockaded at Eshove, without food, munitions or correspondence. The second had to guard Kambulu Camp, General Chelmsford having left to march forward. The Zulus took advantage of that to invade the English camp; we were with the Zulus, as I have already said. The camp was at Isandlwana[30]—an Indian name that I recommend to lovers of Sanskrit.

Cetewayo was in a good enough position to make offers of peace. In his capacity as a savage he was opposed to futile war. His peace offers were therefore made during the first days of July; they failed, of course. I possess a great many details regarding our sojourn at the Cape; I shall put them at the disposal of anyone who wishes. The fake letter attributed to Marcel will serve, for the shame of the forger, as an introduction to the volume I intend to publish. We wrote it together at the Cape of Storms; it bears both our name. It consists of poems, and bears the title Songs of the Sea.

ALBERT NORET

The two associates did not go back to the office of *La Débâcle*, and if they had not been sufficiently unwary

---

[30] The original text has "Bandhlwana," but the copyist or typesetter must have misread the handwriting in Michel's manuscript. I can find no evidence of the name having an origin or meaning in Sanskrit. The events to which Noret refers transpired in 1879, but as we are not told how long before the attempted blackmail these events supposedly occurred, that does not help much to clarify the chronology of the story.

to go there in their own names they would have issued a denial in the matter of the purchase. They would have preferred Albert to summon them before the law, where they would have been able to use their adversary's life of revolt against him, which would have rendered the jury favorable to right-thinking men. The silence of the man who had seen through them weighed upon them.

Albert's article did not surprise anyone; it is on the dead that crows turn; people were disgusted by the slander. However, if it had been the case that no witness had been able to recall the circumstances that had prevented Marcel from being in Paris, how many people would have been duped? Thus is opinion formed!

That particular drama counted for very little at the time of which we are speaking; events were battering at the breach of the entire world.

Even more lost than anyone else in the world were Anna's sons, delivered to Eleazer's widow for the sovereign blackmail on which the two associates were putting their highest hopes. That affair would be a revenge—so much the worse for Roll, for whose return they were on the lookout.

André had not yet been able to talk to the children; he spotted them one morning getting out of a carriage in front of a house of rich appearance, whose outbuildings alone seemed to be inhabited.

Uncle Hymetta showed it to them.

André, drawing close, heard him say to them: "Do you recognize that?"

They blushed and went pale, not daring to rely—but their eyes were involuntarily toward two large windows: those of the Red Room. Hymetta noticed the movement. He would have his revenge.

André understood that the children were serving unwittingly in some shady affair.

The more disquiet Hymetta and Del Mar felt with regard to Albert Noret, the angrier they became with Roll. When the first sled-dog received a whiplash in the land of the polar tribes it bites its neighbor, and reciprocally, all along the team. Thus the wretches were acting in becoming enraged against Roll.

XXIX. Across the Ocean

Roll was in no hurry to come back. Absorbed by the wilderness of waves, and the tempest flapping its wings over the ocean, he forgot his humble individuality. The memoirs that he addressed to learned Societies had lost the character of partiality and taken on a marvelous clarity; it would not have taken much for certain institutes to take them for the last shreds of the veil of the tabernacle; they hastened to promise the scientist all the academic laurels during his lifetime and the Panthéon after his death, in order to get a slight hold on him, but nothing did that.

Roll related the transformations that he saw in nature, in mores, languages and human races, and ended up recognizing that the day was near for the peoples to don virile robes.

He was becoming a revolutionary, it was said. Abbé Cadet had put all his penitents on novenas, and a fast more rigorous than the inhabitants of his colonies, in order to appease the Lord and prevent the scientist from quitting the bosom of the Church or being swallowed up by the cyclones that Wolff depicted so well—but the Lord has always been blind and deaf.

La Débâcle began to reproduce a few passages from Wolff's communications.

None of these things, entirely to the advantage of their project, escaped Hymetta and Del Mar. Like those ancient mythical characters who go forth in threes, sevens or other numbers, they went forth as a pair, always on the lookout. The communality of criminal interests had brought them together; they could no longer break the chain. It was together that they crawled, leaving drool everywhere instead of venom.

They got dirty, not daring to bite, fearful because of the affair of the letters; their fly-paper had been torn by that hornet of a journalist.

Roll was still sailing, exploring unknown archipelagoes in the austral continent that might serve as refuges of humankind, when ours founders. In the study of probabilities past and future, Roll had forgotten himself. The immensity held him; what was he in the universal gravitation, the torments ad cataclysms of worlds? For the moment, the intelligence of the man had stifled the appetites of the wolf.

The learned Socicties had recalled him many times: Roll did not want to come back.

From the austral Ocean he had passed on to the polar lands, recognizing with astonishment, in Josiah's mines and workings, cyclopean endeavors in which the scientist detected scientific means.

Was he dreaming, then? Habituated to so many extraordinary things, was he on the track of the man who sailed the ship without a flag? It was southwards that the brig had headed on emerging from the cyclone.

Roll had reference-points; there was no doubt that he would find the rest. The brig floated in Roll's mind as he had seen it float in the torment. When he had got his teeth into an idea, he shook it furiously, as he would have shaken a prey.

All the way through the polar lands, amid the ice, Roll searched for traces of those who might be extracting sulfur or precious metals. The phantom brig was doubtless crewed by bold companions, taking the wealth of the globe directly. He searched and continued searching, without fear for his own life or those of others.

Luck was with him, as it always was, and carried him through to the end. In a cavity in a rock, a thick sheet of paper, carried by the wind, had remained without the tempest tearing the fragile object apart. Nothing resists destruction better than frailty. The paper has lasted longer than the life of the man from whom the wind had snatched it. It was a map of the coasts of the regions in which he found himself.

That inestimable treasure—for it was traced by a masterly hand—also contained the indication of a maritime route from south to north, with certain places marked, warning of reefs or identifying relief ports.

Roll was holding the thread of the labyrinth. The scientific mission would follow that route.

He took it immediately, instead of wintering in the south, as he had originally intended. His will was law.

XXX. Hymetta's Daughter

Many human wolves have lionesses for daughters. There was never a fresher flower than Hymetta's daughter; her name was Grace, and she bore his surname.

No more magnificent voice ever emerged from the heart and lips of an artiste than that of Grace Hymetta.

Charming, naïve and intelligent, the young woman was adored by her father. It was the only blameless sentiment that the wretch had ever had; by virtue of that alone he was a man.

She loved her father too—but more than anything else, more than art itself, Grace loved the future of humankind.

Hymetta would have had an apoplectic fit if he had know about some of the things his daughter had read, and what she did with what he generously gave her for her meager pleasures.

What Grace read were works by economists giving, without wishing to, every reason to those who wanted everything for everyone. They were books of science, everything in human knowledge that impassions.

The father dealt shamefully in money; the daughter dealt in ideas, science, art and the future. She embraced them with a greater passion.

In Grace's room there were weapons, trophies, red and black banners. She had, for the first time, proudly carried one of those very banners through the battle.

It was in her room, at her piano, that she sang ardent verses:

The blood of the ancestors awakes
An like the sap of spring,
Its waves flow more redly
In the veins of their descendants

Like the sea that extends and rumbles,
Humans, black or white,
Will cover the old world!

It's a legend that is rising
Blowing in the clarions of the wind,
Like the waves, like the tide
The masses are rising in oceans.

Like the sea that extends and rumbles,
Humans, black or white,
Will cover the old world!

Sometimes, by contrast, there were dream-like
lines, which she accompanied with the plash of oars:

Strange flower of the vast waves,
O coral with ruddy branches!
Which covers so many old worlds
And prepares so many new ones.
When, O red-branched coral
Will you elevate new cliffs
Over our imperfect races
For beings that are just and great?

Would Grace not have been the perfect companion
for Jacques the sculptor?

We have related that Hymetta had had the child
during his financial adventures with a Russia woman, to

whom he represented himself as a exile, and whom he had married. She was the only woman he had ever loved. When his frauds were discovered he had fled Moscow, taking his wife and child with him.

The Russian, on learning who her husband really was, had tried to kill herself and little Grace. The child survived.

Hymetta, who was then known as Monsieur le Baron, had changed his nationality; he confided his daughter, with a few thousand francs, to a pious family, who spent the money and made the child, first the rival of its elder daughters, and then the instructress of the younger ones. It was then that Hymetta retrieved her and brought her to Paris, after his most recent escape.

Her father's character had never appeared to Grace in its true light. She knew that he was miserly, but attributed that avarice to the long sequence of bad times that he had suffered—so he said.

Not living in the same wing of the house as the housekeeper and Philippe's children, it took some time for her to become aware of their presence, first seeing Madame Eleazer—the housekeeper, as she was called—coming in, shoving the children before her, heads bowed, eyes ardent, marching along without saying anything.

Grace was horrified by the one, and felt sorry for the others.

"Father," she said, "who are that frightful old woman and those poor children living upstairs?"

"They're orphans that have been entrusted to me."

"And it's to that woman that you've confided them in your turn?"

"She's my housekeeper."

"I don't care about that—I'm only worried about those children."

He dared not refuse his daughter. She had the children brought to her room every day, taught them all that she could, and—most of all—spoiled them.

Grace was twenty; she was beautiful, and the first time one saw her, she made an impression that was never erased.

She had the natural golden hair and steel-blue eyes of Russians. In England she had acquired the freshness of young maidens. In the mornings, her enthusiastic naivety gave her complexion something reminiscent of wild roses.

Finding a resemblance between her and their mother, the children threw their arms around her. She took them in her arms, and from that day on, she had their complete trust.

Then the naïve child achieved with the simplicity of her heart that which Eleazer's widow had been unable to do with all her corruption. She told her father what the children remembered, believing that it would attract a salutary protection to them.

Hymetta was almost remorseful in making use of his daughter's confidence for his intrigues.

As for Eleazer's widow, she said, while darting her viper's tongue over her flat lips: "I don't know what you want to do with those children, but if Mademoiselle Grace gets mixed up in it, the deal will go sour."

Hymetta remained silent.

XXXI. The City in the Ice

Roll's voyage, following the discovery of the map, was a triumph.

Trusting in him, the captain of the ship avoided the smallest reefs, and he identified new harbors in unknown bays.

As if in a dream, Roll followed a wake: that of the Phantom Ship. Standing on deck surveying the expanse, the slowness of the voyage was an anxiety; the fears of his companions relative to the icebergs that were beginning to appear, drifting at the hazards of the currents, seemed paltry to him.

The captain, who had followed Roll's directions, admired his universal knowledge and contemplated with him the bizarre forms of the blocks of ice, some mimicking the porticos of aristocratic houses, others entire cities. Already the coastal glaciers were shining like crystal mountains beneath the halo.

They went through the midst of torments whipping the air and the waves with the noise of cyclones, wintering in a bay marked on the map, further than any other explorer had ventured. Today, that mysterious place, witness to the first attempt on the most terrible land on earth, has returned to the unknown.

Roll was increasingly certain that he would find the nest of the sea-bird for which he was searching there— but, at the same time, he was gripped by a apprehension. What if Jacques, instead of perishing in the waves, had boarded the ship?

Were all the specters of his crime going to return? The only one to whom he gave no thought was his brother; he seemed to be living both their lives at once; that hallucination soothed him.

The route had been quite simple. By way of the Baffin Sea they had entered the strait between Greenland and Washington Land,[31] and passed beyond Cape Britannia; between desolate shores bordered by rocks like giant tombs, they had found a channel free of ice, which did not end and emerged into a sea.

Roll looked at his map anxiously; there was a sign placed over the sea, but nothing further.

With his eyes glued to the sheet that had served him thus far, Roll wondered whether he had struggled so much merely to end up in a sea—a sea that was sometimes free of ice and sometimes completely frozen, according to the season, which made the difference for navigators between land and ocean.

It was a discovery, undoubtedly, but now that the self of the human wolf had reawakened, more terrible than before, he had eyes for nothing but the brig, searching through the unknown, no longer seeing anything but the prey that he was tracking.

Suddenly, it occurred to Roll that one of the openings of the X-shaped sign marked the mouth of the channel extending into the sea. The other opening must be the point for which he was searching.

In the approaches to human agglomerations, a vitality expands into the air; ideas, in passing through it,

---

[31] In fact, "Washington Land" was the name once given to a part of Greenland; the land mass on the other side of the strait at the northern extremity of Baffin Bay (which actually gives access to the Arctic Ocean, although there is no way the author could have known that) is Ellesmere Island—specifically, the part once known as "Grant Land."

leave a magnetic trail. Such was Roll's impression as he went forward, heading due north-west, in the direction of the magnetic pole.

The cold was no more intense than in some regions inhabited by humans. The captain's admiration for the leader of the scientific mission increased; he had foreseen everything.

Suddenly, they thought they saw a mirage—that of a harbor with human habitations.

That harbor was the mouth of the stray arm of the Gulf Stream, which was going to rejoin the steam from which it had branched beneath the waves.

The city was sideways on to that current of warm water, facing an enormous circle of volcanoes sunk in polar cataclysms. The Summer City was sheltered in places by Cyclopean mines; it was constructed so solidly that it resembled the ancient cities of Egypt. Hard labor and united will-power triumphed over the danger of torments by means of that massive architecture.

The other city, deep underground, was a cavern of giants, forging popular thunderbolts for the conquest of universal peace, in which transformations would rapidly be made of humanity, rising, always rising, until the globe grew old and crumbled in space. Those ardent individuals were not content to live differently from their contemporaries; they wanted to hasten the hour of humanity—and for that, they possessed in their arsenal, to be place in the service of right, explosive forces that Gaël claimed to be capable of blowing up the world.

In addition, they had immense wealth and courage, which made every man worth a thousand.

Luck had not deserted Roll; he went from astonishment to astonishment.

The ship that carried him was not alone in the harbor; the colony had a fleet of four brigs at anchor there, constructed in a manner that seemed strange to the new arrivals. Roll understood that various transformations rendered those ships capable of resisting the winds and the sea; for the moment, they were vulgar pontoons making up a dock charged with various cargoes.

On one of those pontoons, black dots were moving back and forth.

The scholars of the scientific mission were contemplating them with profound astonishment, which the black dots verified by successively changing the brig into all the forms it could take in readiness to depart.

It was Josiah and his companions. Suddenly, the ship appeared to them, similar to those of Europe, with cannon to salute friends or enemies, according to the fashion in which the new arrivals presented themselves.

Roll's ship displayed its colors; the brig hoisted its own: a red flag fringed with black.

Astonishment rendered Roll's companions mute; he had but one thought: to destroy this human nest, in which he scented individuals aware of his crime.

It was the first time that strangers had entered the bay; had they come on behalf of the old world, which would only seek to take back this corner of icy land, in order to snuff out the spark of liberty?

Roll introduced himself as an explorer desirous of mapping the coast and recounting the mores of the new world to the old continents.

Josiah and his companions welcomed the new arrivals as brothers. By way of propaganda; they showed them their cities.

Roll understood the enormous achievement of these men, brought together by free association—is not that the effect of universal gravity? He noted everything carefully, including the increase, instead of extinction, of an Inuit tribe that had joined the colony, asking no more at first than to live as they were accustomed to live, and who, instead of being overwhelmed by the superiority of their companions, had gradually entered into their progress, drawn by the attraction that gave them life instead of taking it. He was still thinking, however, of destroying the witnesses to his crime; to reach them, he would have destroyed the world.

For brief moments, he forgot, dazzled, charmed and attracted by his intelligence toward the unexpected endeavors of men who, in science as in mores, had raced ahead. He told himself, too, that from the icy nest they would sink the old world, that it was a danger to order and to the family—but it was for himself alone that Roll was fearful.

"What have you kept of our laws?" he asked Gaël.

"Nothing."

"And what have you made of the family?"

"The difference between a grain of wheat and the sheaf; the family is the society."

"To what fatherland do you belong?"

"To the world; to humankind."

If Roll had not been dragging the ball and chain of his crime, he would have been with them. He also felt attracted by the currents of revolt, hatred and love that were creating another order of being. Momentarily, he lived in liberty, but the hallucination of his crime, whipped up by egotism, stung his face; he had recognized, in an immense studio formed by a cavern, a sculptor working on a full block: the sculptor Jacques.

Jacques also thought that he had recognized him, but his past life now that he was living in the future, seemed to him to be like a soiled item of clothing that he had once worn and dragged through the gutter, no longer part of himself.

Roll's resolution was made; the colony would perish. He was going to verify the savage proverb that the foot of a European never treads on new ground without desiccating it.

The means that Roll would employ to destroy the icy haven were undecided, but he would certainly do the job himself. Why confide his project to someone else, in order to be betrayed? He felt that he was big enough to take care of his business himself.

Out there, beneath the snowstorms, that handful of free-living people was dreaming of the liberation of the world.

Roll was dreaming of the destruction of the colony.

The members of the scientific mission were received cordially, but an involuntary mistrust enveloped them. They felt it, and were astonished by it—except for Roll, who abandoned and reformulated a hundred plans of destruction, one after another. The principal ship the *Étoile*, was to winter in the colony—bad news for those whose sense of smell was good.

Roll, in particular, gave the impression of a domesticated reptile that could not be entirely trusted. Madame Basis suspected him of all kinds of evil designs against Dr, Gaël, but she was accustomed to no one listening to her.

Jacques kept an eye on the man with the bright eyes.

But one does not throw into the water, with stones around their necks, like mad dogs, people who are on a scientific mission, especially when one is seeking to agitate the idea of Justice before the entire world. Roll would have merited it, though.

As for the captain of the *Étoile*, like the rest of the mission, he had no inkling at all of the crime that Roll was planning.

The entire colony drew its water from snow or melted ice via its alembics. He thought about poisoning that water, or the beverages bought In Europe by Josiah; it would not have been difficult for him to procure what he needed to make poisons from the laboratories, but he wanted the catastrophe to be instantaneous. The colonists lived, alone in families or in groups, in immense subterranean halls; meals could not take place at the same time; the first ones attained would be able to obtain help from the others.

Perhaps he could make use of explosives.

Roll became enthusiastic about each project, and then, when the time came to put it into action, he saw its impossibilities. He could not blow up the caverns like a lump of rock, he thought.

The more time passed, the more his hatred grew. In consequence of the danger that his crime might be discovered, he had embraced in his dread everything that he saw in himself with disgust. He was about to act with the rage of the old world against the new.

An unexpected discovery gave him a new idea.

The regular movement of the waters beating the shore made him think that if he could contrive an opening, the sea would rush into the caverns and inundate them. In order to make that opening, he would blow up a few rocks.

But there too the impossible presented itself. At the noise of the detonation, the colony would be on its feet, and the damage countered.

He hoped that the breach in the rock might not be the only destruction; would not every fall of rock in these regions lead to other collapses? But the project still seemed impossible to him. He had once sunk the *Whole*, though; he ought to be able to sink the colony. It was the same thing, on a larger scale.

Wolff became careworn, which the captain and the others attributed to his scientific preoccupations, but the colony was beginning to divine some malevolent design.

Josiah, to whom the wolfish face seemed to resemble that of the passenger on the *Whole*, Jacques and Jean Hénoe, were of the opinion that when one finds a scorpion one steps on it—but a man's life requires that one should be certain of the truth before taking action. They had to be sure before making certain that he could do no harm.

Roll could not go to the extremity of the caverns without arousing suspicion. Like the mines of the Black Country, they extended over an immense territory. He could not ask any more questions; it was necessary for him to wait. Would luck cease to favor him?

No, fate did not abandon him. Cataclysms had disrupted the ground, bringing to the surface what should have been beneath, and that which should have been far away closer to hand. For that reason, a stream of naphtha ran through one of the upper caverns to fall into another; they made use of it without danger: Roll would make arrangements to the contrary.

The deep strata that had been disturbed had more resources for destruction than for life.

The colonists made use of the force of tempests as an instrument; it was necessary that they should not be alerted. Thus, Roll continued searching. What he was sure of was that if he could cause the colony to perish, the ice would close over its tomb like the waves.

In addition to ordinary labors, groups of artists of all kinds had formed in the caverns. Some came together into choirs or orchestras, other for sculpture, enormous blocks being sculpted by groups into statues and monuments. Broadly-drawn frescos covered the walls, and, seen in the electric light, of which they made use in preference, delighted by their grandiose of terrible expression. For the most part, they were scenes of polar nature or human misery, which everyone had seen on the old continents.

In a natural basin whose depth was unknown, boats moved back and forth without dread to reach the other side of the lake, where enormous statuettes formed endless colonnades.

How had that polar land been disturbed?

Sometimes, Roll made notes vaguely on the manipulations made by tempests; then the obsession returned. How could they be caused to perish, all at once?

The first time that he heard the waves so close to the caverns he had thought of blowing up the wall; he came back to that idea incessantly.

The general suspicion of Wolff might have turned into certainty one night.

Under the pretext of carrying out maneuvers, he made all of his party embark on the *Étoile*. The thing had been done almost naturally, but those who had already encountered Roll scented danger. The danger did, indeed exist, but not where they saw it.

Gaël, Josiah, Jacques, Jean Hénoe and the two Miralowski brothers went on to one of their pontoons, and watched the *Étoile*'s maneuvers from there. There was nothing unusual. The *Étoile* tried out the same apparatus as the colony's ships. That was flattering for Josiah; it did not make him more suspicious.

While they were observing the *Étoile*, the watch in the caverns had been organized in groups, according to occupations and characters, all perfectly tranquil in the presence of death.

In Gaël's grotto, Madame Basis, Jabouille[32] and his wife, who were at the same intellectual level but played their part nevertheless, had come together to chat around the hearth. The canaque Daga and the gentleman who declared himself to be politically neutral had found a center of attraction there. These simple souls who, following their intelligence, stretched themselves out in the sun of liberty, warming themselves happily, could not do otherwise.

In the midst of a profound silence, Daga recounted in his shrill voice, slightly rusted by the extreme difference in climate, how he had been condemned back home.

A man of his tribe had committed some misdemeanor or other. He was taken in his stead and interrogated. Daga only knew a few words of French and did not understand what was being asked of him. He had confessed without being aware of it—but he did not regret having lived with the refugees, for he had never seen so many beautiful things in his own land. However, he dreamed continually about the bright moonlight filter-

---

[32] Readers familiar with *The Human Microbes* will remember Jabouille, but might be surprised to find him here as the supposedly-dead Josiah, given that—unlike Julius, the O'Patricks and others unmentioned in the present texts, who were determined to escape from New Caledonia, he had expressed his intention of staying where he was

ing through the branches, about niaoulis[33] raising their wind-tormented branches, and especially about his old father, from whom he had been separated; he was undoubtedly dead by now.

Madame Basis, who was tranquilly pursuing her own train of thought, declared that she had a poor opinion of the presence of the chief of the mission, who was always prowling around them. She had just seen him slipping into the caverns while his comrades, on his orders, were aboard their ship. That man definitely ought to be closely watched, and, if necessary, sacrificed for the sake of general security. That was Gaël's opinion, the good woman added, sententiously.

"Bah!" said the prisoner who eschewed politics. "One man can't do anything against us. Let me tell you a story. I haven't told it yet.

"The first time I was arrested, it was outside a public meeting; they were making arrests at random. I was just passing by, but the agents, frightened, said that I had assaulted them. Why would I have done that—given that I was alone and they were occupying the entire street? I had an open pen-knife in my pocket; it was said that I had struck blows with a dagger. I was given a month in prison. That made me angry: I was a prisoner of the State. Except that, as I was a royalist, when I got out, I wanted to fight for the king. You can see that I wasn't very advanced in those days.

"Wanting to bring off a big coup all on my own, I said to each of my comrades: 'If you don't do what I say, quickly and well, I'll make use of papers, compromising for you, that I have in my bag. While swearing

---

[33] The original text misrenders the name of this tree as *maouli*; it is also known as the Broad-Leafed Paper-Bark.

fidelity to the king, you've solicited something from the Republic!'

"My fellows, of course, all had something for which to reproach themselves, for they were always trotting out propaganda for the king. One day, though, a big Breton came to find me so that I could show the bag at a public meeting. He'd promised to break my back if I didn't do it. I took an old black bag that was at hand and followed him to the place where the meeting was being held. I tried to get away all along the route, but it wasn't possible. We arrived—me, the bag and the Breton. There were a lot of people at the meeting who didn't want to be there any more than I did. They were afraid that someone would find something out, and I was scared because they wouldn't find anything.

"The big fellow had escaped from a heap of earwigs that fell on the head of an old countess. I was doomed. Those who had trembled had brought me there. I was had up for blackmail, fraud and so on, and I got five years. That bored me; I wanted to leave for Caledonia to sniff the air. You know the rest."

There was a moment of merriment, but they were feeling drowsy. They were about to leave in order to go to bed when a small sound, like a splash, was heard. Doubtless it was the sea in the distance.

Yes, it was the sea, but it was very close at hand.

Roll had employing all his means at the same time; he had just blown up the wall that would give the sea access to the first grottoes, and he had set fire to the naphtha well. Stifling vapors were already spreading.

Getting up in haste, the unfortunates fell back heavily, choked by the emanations.

The peninsula collapsed in part, causing immense and furious jets of water to spring from the ocean depths, which rose up as far as the thick red clouds amassed by the detonations.

The catastrophe ran its course.

Thus were thousands of men swallowed up, along with marvels of art and new inventions. Nothing survived that was buried beneath the watery shroud of that new Pompeii.

Jacques, Jean Hénoe and the brothers Miralowski, observing on their ships, were subjected to an enormous thrust toward the open sea, but they came back once the darkness of the blown-up caverns had dissipated somewhat.

They had been mistake; the danger had been in the colony itself.

When they were able to land on the shore, horribly pitted, the seething sea was extended over the buried grottoes.

The *Étoile* had been subjected to the same thrust, and was sailing in open water, where Roll was able to enjoy the terrible spectacle in safety.

Gaël's grotto, exploding like a shell, caused the waves to tremble over a vast distance, so many chemical products had been accumulated there.

Further detonations followed; they were the stories of dynamite and picrate, which exploded along with new products whose secret was lost. Not all of them, however; the terrible product on which Gaël was counting to put an end to war, which had no other name but gaëlite, had been placed by the terrible inventor in a cavern some distance away from the rest. That one alone remained; in taking from it the explosives with which he did his work, Roll had forgotten to leave what was required to destroy it. He had also neglected the formula, which he could have stolen from Gaël. It did not matter to him, provided that the colony was destroyed, that the colors of which Gaël made use remained on the bottom like a heap of corn. Everything there was intact: the retorts, the stone troughs in which metal cooled and the washing-basins were all there. On the ground there were little yellow pools in which a greenish scum floated.

A stone vat, a natural curiosity of the grotto, which had been holed for the preparation, was intact, the crystals heaped up in natural hollows in the rock; a mass of sulfur remained among the rare survivors.

Jacques, Gaël and a few others gazed at the disaster.

Jacques had difficult in repressing his grief for so many brave men buried, so many inventions destroyed. Gaël stood up to his full height Even though nothing was left of all that, he displayed his forehead, still as pale as death, still arrogant; the idea would live.

For several days they searched the tongue of land, battered by the advancing waves, from top to bottom. Everywhere there was the debris of industry and art. On the third day, a few cadavers were washed up by the sea. Gaël recognized Madame Basis; clasped to her chest she was holding a little copper casket in which the notes of is discovery were locked.

"Poor, dear, dead woman," said the old man—and then repented of his compassion. "Forward!" he cried.

They threw themselves into the waves, toward the brigs, which had suffered no damage. Roll was setting sail for Europe, on the rim of the horizon.

The cadavers yielded up by the water already numbered several hundred. Josiah, Jacques and their companions had already given up hope of finding a single living soul when the canaque Daga appeared from the maze of subterranean tunnels. Exhausted he had no more understanding of how he had been able to escape than he had had of his condemnation.

The survivors of the disaster thus numbered seven: Josiah, Gaël, Jacques, Jean Hénoe, Daga and the brothers Miralowski.

Having buried their dead, they thought about returning to the ships. On examining the vessels, they discovered Roll's final crime. He had tried to blow up the flotilla, but had bungled a part of the preparations.

The engulfing of the caverns was entered by the *Étoile*'s captain in his log as a geological event, from which the wreckage of the colonists' ships followed naturally; it was a true miracle that the *Étoile* had not perished.

"If they haven't discovered our secrets of fabrication," Gaël said, "we can take on the entire world."

It was with that very product that Roll had been able to bring down the enormous masses now beneath the waves.

They had one stroke of luck. A tempest raking the sea-bed threw up on the coast two boxes containing their maps and marine instruments. Josiah noticed attempts to perforate the hulls of the vessels, which had not succeeded because of the hardness of their armor. He understood the loss of the *Whole*.

In spite of the pontoons' armor, plates had been loosened. Roll had not had the patience to continue.

What idea led them not to follow in the bandit's footsteps?

The trial had been decisive for Gaël's explosive—and decisive, above all, for the colony, since it had been able to succeed in the most unfavorable conditions. They agreed to make a second attempt in the unknown lands of Africa. Thanks to the fertility of nature the success would be more rapid; they had no time to spare.

In Europe, cyclones were being unleashed: cyclones of states, of ideas, of the ground; an entire renewal of the Earth; the Eocene of the sphere and humankind.

XXXII. In France

Roll had returned to France before them, covered in glory, having sailed from the south to the north more rapidly than anyone in the world; having passed through the Baffin Strait they had found a peninsula in an open sea inhabited by "an Inuit tribe" joined by a few Europeans. These people, living in caverns, had been obliterated by a catastrophe, the wall preserving them having collapsed. Thanks to skillful maneuvers, the *Étoile* had escaped the violence of the tidal wave. It had been protected from all eventualities by new apparatus, which transformed it, according to the peril, into an armored box, a balloon or a ship.

The account of the voyage impassioned public opinion—most of all, Hymetta and Del Mar. The greater Wolff's glory was, the more fecund their blackmail would be. It was their revenge. The lesson administered by *La Débâcle*, however, had been carried far and wide, and that rendered them pensive. If anyone discovered what they were doing, they were lost—and they would, indeed, have been if Roll's terrible passions had come into play.

Hymetta, in absolute control by virtue of the children's memories, which his daughter relayed to him innocently, resolved to attempt a decisive coup. Grace, however, had been sad for several days; although the entirety of what Hymetta called "business" did not feel the world trembling, Grace sensed the immense revolution.

Hazard, as usual, was moved to take a hand in events.

Having taken the children out, Grace wanted to distract them, and also to find out why her father was so interested in them. Should he not be occupied with his own business, forgetting theirs? Poor Grace was far from the truth.

The children were not growing much, and did not know very much; without the affection they had for Grace they would have died, not drawing life from anywhere.

"Why were you entrusted to my father?" the young woman asked. She had not previously thought of asking them that question.

The idea that he had represented himself as their uncle astonished Grace; perhaps they really were relatives, but the mysterious procedures worried her. The presence of the "housekeeper" also worried her; that horrible creature, who outdid the financier in avarice, seemed to her to be deadly. It was necessary that the associates give in to the young woman, who no longer wanted to see the sinister face of the housekeeper. She knew the role that the old shrew had played with regard to the children and questioned them continually. They were terrified of her, and did not want to say anything.

Grace recalled the insistence with which her father also interrogated her; she shivered, thinking about Hymetta's associate, the frightful dwarf, whom she had seen going into the office. She had been afraid that he might see her, without knowing why.

Having brought the children back, she went to see Hymetta.

"Father," she said, "you love me, don't you?"

He held out his two claw-like hands, almost with tears in his eyes. No one would have recognized the financier, of whom it was said derisively that he had a "heart of gold." It was, indeed, made of gold.

"What do you want?" he asked, affectionately.

"You're rich, even for someone who holds on to his money. Well, it's necessary to get out of the association with your gnome. Get rid of that old magpie of a house-keeper, and let's live, just the two of us, without all this bother. I'll devote myself to my music, and we'll be happy. But right away, Father—immediately, you under-stand—it's necessary to put an end to the affair involv-ing the two children."

Hymetta let her say that without any interruption. Something rose into this throat, choking him.

What did Grace know? How could he separate him-self from Del Mar?

"Listen," he said. "The only thing I can do right away is to get rid of Madame Eleazer. As for the chil-dren, I can't do that. We'll see."

"Soon, Father? Won't you?"

"Yes, soon."

Madame Eleazer's astonishment was great when she learned that she was being dismissed, under the pre-text of attempting another education for the children. She would get her due.

The old woman had sniffed a fruitful affair; she wanted her share of it, and demanded compensation. Having left a good position she was being left on the pavement, excluded from magnificent speculations, etc.

She went to find Del Mar, and told him that she did not believe him to be party to Hymetta's caprice.

He seized the perfidious excuse. "Indeed," he said. "The blow came from Hymetta's daughter."

"That stuck-up little prude! I suspected as much."

"Keep that to yourself, my dear lady. It's necessary to know who our enemies are."

"I'm grateful, and ready to return the favor."

Madame Eleazer carried everywhere with her, like a part of her carapace, an enormous basket containing her personal possessions—which is to say, a pan in which to make sugared wine, a pack of tarot cards, an old headscarf that had lasted her thirty years, and a number of perfume-bottles.

Her anger was so great that she forgot it when she left.

"Worse luck for the child," said Del Mar, putting the basket into a corner of his lumber-room. "Madame Eleazer will be back."

Del Mar's anticipation was accurate.

Once she was outside, the shrew realized that she did not have her basket, her headscarf, her cards and her bottles.

Bah! she said to herself. *I'll come back for them.*

She bought another old shawl at the second-hand shop in order to look more respectable, and went back to the house to which the children had been taken. Madame Eleazer did not keep her eyes or ears in her pocket; she had followed them at a distance. Chance procured her a favorable entrance.

To distract himself, Roll ordered that the old woman who was asking for him so insistently be admitted, but he found nothing in it but annoyance. He did not like sinister faces, and the old woman's displeased him.

With her eyes hidden by her spectacles and her spectacles hidden by the brim of a think black bonnet, along with her vulgar and horrible head, the window Eleazer scented the reek of crime. Her dirty paws protruded from the edge of her shawl like those of a bat; one might have thought she was looking for a place from which to hang.

Roll gave her a sign to sit down.

"I've come to warn you about a great danger," the old woman began.

"I'm not worried about dangers."

"Monsieur le Juge, you don't know me, and you're not obliged to believe me, but if something were to happen to you…! You don't know who the enemies are who are pursuing you: implacable enemies: the two partners of the Banque de Fumosas, and especially Hymetta's daughter. When you want to know more, here's my address: Lady Companion, Poste Restante, Bureau de la Place Blanche, initials J.B."

Half-farcical and half-strange, the old lady's speech awoke an aguish in Roll.

"Do you need a handout? Why employ these threats, which can't frighten me?"

"Do you remember the Red Room, Monsieur le Juge?"

Roll went pale. The old lady withdrew without saying any more, happy to depart on the effect of those words.

For several days, he had the horrible old woman before his eyes. He sensed her slithering like a viper around him; he heard her words: "Do you remember the Red Room?"

That torture became so terrible that he resolved to see the reality face to face. Chance, as usual, threw it in his face.

At that time, the opera *Les Druides*[34] was being staged: choirs of bards accompanied by the lute; sacrifices in the forests; ballets of poulpiquets[35] on the deserted heath; a choir of druidesses accompanied by an imitation of the sound of waves. That stage-set reeked of verbena and gorse, as refreshing as the shade of oaks.

Every evening, the Opéra was overflowing, from the principal boxes to the seamstress's cubby-hole, from which one looked down on the stage.

Roll took it into his head to go and see *Les Druides*.

The first scene is grandiose and calm; at a crossroads in the forest, by moonlight, the brave men of Armorica swear to die for the deliverance of Gaul. A lute solo is heard in the depths of the woods.

Roll felt a great peace descend upon him. He became thoughtful, while the strings of the lute emitted notes like rain, drop by drop.

Harmony extends far beyond our miseries, our crimes, our fatalities; its thought goes much further than our languages can say, which lack words for the things we feel without understanding them, like colors to the blind. Roll lived the harmony.

In a box opposite was a young blonde woman whose thick hair was reminiscent of an unbound wheatsheaf, also listening enraptured. Two children with

---

[34] There really is a French opera by Ignace Seyfried called *Les Druides* (1801), but the one than the author has in mind is far more likely to be Vicenzo Bellini's "Druid opera" *Norma* (1831), which was much more famous and successful. Richard Wagner added an aria to it for an 1837 production, and Louise Michel was a great admirer of Wagner.

[35] Poulpiquets are one of the numerous subspecies of the Breton "little people," not much, if any, different from korrigans.

ardent eyes were clinging to her closely, charmed and dazzled. Roll thought he was seeing the specter of Anna bringing forth his children, in order that they could call him "murderer" before the entire audience! He thought about Hymetta's daughter, and the old woman's words "Do you remember the Red Room?"

That horrible net closed around him.

The children had seen him too; they threw themselves backwards. "There!" they whispered to Grace.

Roll, retreating into a corner of the box, watched them without being seen.

At the exit from the theater, wanting to see the specter again and finish with it, he followed the carriage that took the young woman away. It really was the enemy of whom the old woman had spoken, Grace Hymetta, the banker's daughter.

How did she come to resemble Anna? Did the dead return with a spectral rejuvenation?

XXXIII. The Amours of a Wolf

Stronger than anything in the world was the insensate love with which Roll was smitten for that phantom of Anna, appearing to him as a harbinger of doom.

He wanted to see her again; it would not be difficult for him to destroy those around her who might be able to defend her. Had he not destroyed a colony, a world?

He wrote to the widow Eleazer. What did it matter? The woman could give him details that he needed.

Grace, habituated to liberty in England, where she had been brought up, often went out alone. She went to lectures, to plays, to the poor quarters and to meetings, sometimes returning in a carriage and sometimes on foot, scarcely paying any heed to the weather and even less to the time.

The men she met in these various places treated her as a comrade; she was an intelligence, an artiste.

"These details are indifferent to me," said Roll to Madame Eleazer. "I wanted to see whether you were telling the truth I'll have you summoned when I need you."

He gave her a hundred francs, thus disposing her to give him as much information, true or false, as he might wish.

Roll's decision was made; he would abduct the young woman. She would be his, dead or alive. That was all the same to him; he wanted Grace. After that, the universe could fall apart.

The opportunity was not long in arriving.

It was an evening at the end of May, similar to the one on which Roll had committed his fratricide.

There was revolution in the air; a war of potentates had gone awry; they were going back into their shells while the human crowds amassed, driven by the secular spring.

Grace thought about the infinite number of children thus abandoned, perhaps more so than the ones with whom she was occupied. She said to herself: *It's not just two that it's necessary to save, but all of them.*

She sensed the hour approaching.

But she did not carry the flag of the starvelings in the revolt, for she was dead before it arrived.

One evening, when she had gone out alone and was coming back thoughtfully, as was her custom, it was late. Grace was not giving any thought to bandits prowling around her. Her march was rhythmic, as to the beat, as if to the beat of a subterranean drum.

Roll saw her pass by, even more beautiful because of the thoughts that buoyed her up. He thought about Valkyries, and that was how she appeared to him.

The night was advanced, no one was about any longer; he had high hopes for that night.

"Be careful, Grace," one of her friends had said to her. "An evil-looking man is following you." But she had taken a small revolver from her pocket and showed it to him, laughing.

She had just turned into the dark Rue Daubenton, leading to the Pitié's halls of the dead.[36] Grace liked to walk on her own like that through the sinister darkness.

---

[36] This reference is presumably to the Cimetière Saint-Médard, whose gate is at one end of the Rue Daubenton, where it intersects with the Rue Mouffetard. There was a convent of the Filles de la Charité associated with the Église Saint-Medard, supervised for some time in the 19th century by Soeur Rosalie

Roll judged the moment propitious, threw himself upon her like a wolf and carried her off.

He had pounced on his prey so precipitately that she already had a handkerchief in her mouth and could not break the grip of the muscular arms that were bearing her away.

Perceiving that she was lost, she succeeded in pulling out her revolver and pulling the trigger. It did not matter much to her whether it was her or the bandit that perished; either way, she would be saved.

It was her.

Covered in blood, as Pierre had been, Roll was surrounded by twenty people brought running by the sound of the shot. When they took the woman covered in blood from Roll's arms, they also kept hold of him.

He did not try to run away, overwhelmed by the horror, the blood and the May night, which brought back his phantoms.

The street was so dark, the street-lights so wan, that the scene was not revealed in all its horror until the arrival of lanterns.

Grace was recognized. A student who encountered her often—the same one who had told her to be careful—recognized Roll as the individual who had been following her. The latter, however, recovering his presence of mind, looked them in the face.

"I picked this woman up just as everyone came. I don't know who shot her. I wanted to save her." And, taking cards from his pocket, he added: "I'm Philippe Wolff!"

Rendu, one of the founders of the Societé de Saint-Vincent-de-Paul, with whose work Louise Michel would have been very familiar.

The crowd parted respectfully, seeking to knock down the student who had brought the accusation. A few cried: "Hurrah for Philippe Wolff!"

"You're free, Monsieur," said the police commissaire who was summoned. "If the law has need of your testimony, you'll be called."

Could so famous a scholar have committed such a crime?

Roll went back home, ready to fight anyone. He was gripped by rage, his furious teeth eager to bite.

XXXIV. The Father

Grace's death, announced to Hymetta the next morning, struck him like a thunderbolt. Then the thought of vengeance possessed him entirely. To avenge his daughter was almost to bring her back of life.

Del Mar, however hard his heart was, supported him on this occasion, when they would have everything against them and nothing in their favor.

There are people over whom accusation slides; Roll was one of them. People were appalled by the insult to the scholar and magistrate.

In addition to the young man who had recognized Roll, others would similarly recognize the man who was following Grace—otherwise, Roll would have caused the accusation to fall upon his accuser, the student who had been the first to come forward.

Hymetta also had the help of finance, and made use of it.

There was almost a possibility of putting the famous and honored Wolff on trial. That caused an enormous sensation, but no one took the view that he should be put in detention.

He was free, and the affair might not have had any further consequences, without Madame Eleazer's hatred for the young woman. Her death could not make her forget that Grace had got her sacked, and it occurred to her that she could help Wolff with information, so she went to his house.

They made an agreement that she would bring him more, and, finding herself well paid in addition to the triumph of her hatred, she resolved to stir things up by returning to her former place of employment. The circumstance of her basket, which he had the well-known mania of carrying around, furnished her with the opportunity.

Having gone to visit Del Mar, who handed over the object without going into as much detail as she would have wished, the old woman pushed audacity as far as going to see Hymetta under the pretext of offering him her condolences.

The latter, who was having Roll's house watched, knew about her acquaintance with him.

As soon as the old woman opened her mouth he knew that his daughter's blood was on her hands, and, losing his head in his fury, he threw her out of the room, and shut the heavy oak door behind her.

Thinking that the thing that caught in the door was the old lady's basket, Hymetta leaned on it pitilessly— but it was not the basket; it was the old woman herself, whose head was slowly crushed.

It was necessary to explain that death in the investigation that followed Hymetta's arrest. Del Mar, foreseeing that other things than the death of the old woman would be discovered, fled with as much gold as he could carry.

There was a link between Roll and the affair; there was no doubt that the old wma had been to Roll's house; she had been seen there several times. He descended slowly into scorn, his ermine robe trailing in the blood— but there was a turnabout; a few repressions having taken place, many people leaned in the other direction.

After all, if Wolff was holding the young woman in his arms, it was because he had helped her before anyone else. Everything rendered the eminent man unassailable. The old woman might have been some beggar.

Soon, the fault weighed entirely upon Grace. Was she not the daughter of a Greek, a man of whom everyone said, now, that instead of stealing from imbeciles he was attacking the honor of an immortal. Student comrades of Grace and a host of other ill-famed individuals testified in vain that the young woman merited respect. As for the press, which was astonished by the liberty afforded to Roll, those people merited accusation more than he did; the editor of *La Débâcle* had already been given six months in prison and a thousand-franc fine, having advanced deceitful accusations for political reasons.

Grace's body, exposed at the Morgue beneath the gilded sheaf of her hair, attracted crowds.

The autopsy demonstrated that the shot had been fired in circumstances that exonerated Roll completely. The affair changed direction; he was the one who became the victim.

The shot had been fired when the young woman had fallen; that fall had taken place in unknown circumstances, for which Roll could not be responsible. It was beyond doubt that he had picked her up in order to help her. The suggestion of an abduction could only have come from fomenters of disorder.

In prison, Hymetta thought of nothing but the death of his child; the rest hardly mattered to him. Only the father survived the collapse.

Philippe's children, in the upheaval caused by the death of Grace and that of old Madame Eleazer, owed it to André's presence of mind—he took them away—that they were not sent back to the penitentiary colony. They were no more fortunate for that, the poor mites.

XXXV. The End of a Wolf

The arrival in Europe of Josiah, with his companions, escaped from disaster, was a *coup de théâtre*.

The murderous assault mounted on the very place where nature itself would have been an obstacle for any other society, and Gaël's discoveries, centuries ahead of those of Europe, like everything that is true, met with a great deal of incredulity.

The simplicity of the life that the refuges had led, having no other law than that of the universe in their harsh corner of the earth, everyone committed to the happiness of all, was, many people said, a utopia, even though it had been actual. The wind that seeps away dead institutions had never blown so strongly, never heaped up so many ruins. Young bourgeois had never been more swollen with terror. Popular tempests were blowing thunderously.

Such was the hour when Roll's case, dismissed and forgotten on the part of the law, was concluded before a different tribunal.

He had always had unusual luck.

Protected by a defense whose rationale was his qualities as a magistrate and scholar, Roll owed his salvation primarily to that mask, and so long as he was Philippe, he was inviolable.

Anna, escaped from the lunatic asylum, had shared the burden of poverty with her companion at the house on the Colombes road. A little hard and ill-paid work permitted them to have respectable clothes and a shelter, but only Anna survived.

Left alone, having no other thought than that of her children, she concealed her identity, awaiting the hour of justice.

But who told her that justice would come? Has the hour ever come, since the time when the appeal was made?

Yes, sometimes it has come, only to disappear again.

That day, it showed itself again; no one knew whether it would be forever, or only to depart again.

The crowd had Paris, and after the victory there was an immense calm. What were they going to do, under the hot pressure of the idea?

By comparison with the human transformation in process, the destiny of a few unfortunate poor people hardly mattered.

Germinal was sowing its seeds, and without anger, by necessity, the old stubble was being torn up.

Everywhere, unconsciously driven by the moment, human groups were forming, beginning to move around one another: a human gravitation similar to stellar gravitation, which will be the order of tomorrow, the order of liberty and individual conscience. But the tomorrow of which they was so much talk, which was frightening, being only a beginning, was interrupted by breakdowns, one after another, and sometimes several together.

By virtue of one of the troubled blasts of that first moment in which the effluvia of spring rose up, a horrible and sinister procession traversed Paris toward the Seine.

A tall man, his clothes in shreds, his wolf-like hair bristling on his enormous skull, fled straight ahead.

"To the water! To the water!" howled furious voices, and he went toward the water, as if it were summoning him.

The prisons had been opened; that is always the first idea. That was how Hymettus had got out.

Then, the father had resumed his pursuit of the man who had caused his child's death.

Anna was also searching, wanting to avenge her children. Hymetta and Anna had encountered one another, and had cried: "Justice! Justice!"—and the crowd had invaded Roll's house. He fled before the gale of anger.

"To the water! To the water!"

Roll was on the quays, one the side where old Notre-Dame, the Palais de Justice and the Prefecture are situated.

A street-urchin had the idea, without quite knowing why, of going up to the belfry of the old church and sounding the knell; night had come.

Then, under the funereal plaint, like a hunted wolf, Roll leapt on to the parapet, stood their momentarily, and fell like a stone.

The water splashed under the muted impact.

At the same moment, without anyone knowing who was responsible, an edifice was surrounded by a circle of flames, and a red cock crowed the morning.

Far higher than the flame soared liberty; the new legend had risen, marching in the epic: the immense epic sung by all voices, respired by all breasts. One might have thought that a thousand epochs had gone by.

Then, after that human wave biting the old shore, the popular tide drew back, a long, long way, and one might have thought that one was living backwards—but the tidal wave returned, and bit much deeper.

XXXVI. The Debacle

When the sea-beds shift, the summits of mountains become islands, and corals build reefs on the slopes where goats once grazed.

Nature is harmonized on new bases; no debris of the old order any longer has its employ. They are broken intervals, notes lost from a scale. Sometimes the march of progress is fearfully slow, but it is sure.

After the isolated human beast the flock is coming. It is time for free humans on the free earth.

The forms that will be effaced in the catastrophe cling on to existence; unlike animals, which forget their ferocity during catastrophes, the voracity of human devourers is augmented as the flood rises.

The vampire, and the octopus attached to its prey by all the suckers of all its tentacles, are less avid than a human beings of the old order of things, in the grip of all their appetites.

The danger that causes ferocity to become dormant in beasts arouses it in humans. During the fire at the Opéra-Comique,[37] brutes were seen to stab women who got in their way.

The conclusion of this book is a fraction of the debacle, with its struggles of wild beasts in peril, and the pallor of first light reddening the dawn of the new day.

The Nevsky Prospekt, especially, is in celebration, the sole tree of liberty that has yet been planted in Rus-

---

[37] Presumably the fire of 25 May 1887, in which 84 people died

sia—the gallows—will bear fruit today: beautiful fruit swollen with sap, for the crows to eat.

Around the citadel is the broad and deep waters of the Neva; the approach to it appears so impossible that it tempts audacity; a thousand extra precautions are taken, but the increased precautions are unnecessary; the bridges are bordered with soldiers like parapets.

The entire semicircle of the Voznesensky Prospekt is full; its bastions are covered. The Gargarine Quay has its line of barracks; the drill field and the Summer Gardens are swarming with uniforms.

There is a whole set of palaces to guard: the Palace of Tauride and the Convent of Smolensk are heaving with troops.

The muzjiks, in festival costume, pass as best they can between the carriages, some of which are closed, containing important State dignitaries who like to see without being seen.

From the citadel, along the broadest and longest roads, over the Troitsky bridge and the streets alongside the Summer Gardens, the Mikhailovsky Palace and the Nevsky Prospekt, three young men are being transported through the city of the Tsar, the father of Russia, to the gallows.

There had originally been some thought of making them disappear without a fuss; they had been put in the citadel in order that it might absorb them, like so many others of whom no news was ever heard, but a need to spread fear had been felt. People were beginning to say that from the depths of the citadel, one could communicate with the city, with Russia, and with the world, and that one could emerge from their alive. In order to silence the legend, the government had set up the gallows in public.

That was the worst means of making friends for the Tsar and the best of obtaining that silence known as order, in which, brooded by death, conspiracies are born and grow.

From the portrait of George,[38] rotated by a button in the Alexander Square, to the citadel and the various palaces, those of whom the Tsar is sure—which is to say, those whose lives depend on the existence of the Tsar—can circulate around the city.

That is a reason for the Tsar's enemies to do the same.

Thus, in the branches and twigs of St. Petersburg, as elsewhere, the hunters and the hunted—the dogs of the pack, the beaters and the prey—cross one another's paths.

Today, there are eighteen who appear before the councils of war; at that time there were only three; it was the doubly matinal hour of the dawn of the day and the awakening of liberty.

They wanted to stifle that awakening.

The condemned, as always, were marching proudly, raising their heads in which the idea was flamboyant in their eyes, open to the future. They were marching in the resplendence that death made them see more closely.

Having arrived at the Alexander Square, the preparations for the execution appeared to them without troubling them. People are used to such things out there; they d not trouble anyone. The killing-machine is sim-

---

[38] King George I of Greece married the Grand Duchess Olga Constantinova in the Winter Palace over looking Palace Square (which must be what the author means by "Alexander Square") in 1867, so he is presumably the person depicted in this (presumably fictitious) rotting portrait.

ple: a platform, which will be withdrawn for the execution, is surmounted by the gallows, the ropes hanging down therefrom, swaying gently in the wind. A crow hungrier than the others is perched on the crossbar, awaiting the fruits to savor; the rest of the flock are perched in the trees of the Prospekt.

To the soldiers who have come by visible routes are added others who have come in secret by the passage leading from the portrait of King George to the citadel, to the public squares, to the countryside, etc.

Strung out among the muzjiks are the companions of those about to be hanged, a few of them having come by mysterious routes, others with the crowd. They want to be seen by those who are going to die. As for learning themselves how one dies, does one not know that, when one has a human heart?

The condemned are thinking about those who have preceded them.

After the black period of thirty years—the deathlike sleep of bloody White Russia—the awakening had taken place; there was new blood to shed for liberty.

Hertzen, Bakunin, Lermontov and Pushkin had sounded the wake-up call, and now the idea was growing, filling with its fiery breath Nikolayev, Straede and so many others, those of Siberia, Nitcheve corresponding from the ravine of the fortress through all the Tsar's police.[39] That story revivified them, as if, so close to

---

[39] The last three names are unfamiliar, and do not seem to correspond to those of any prominent nihilists or *narodniki*—but Paris was host to many Russian exiles in the 1880s, and Louise Michel would have heard of many whose names remained relatively esoteric.

death, they had a better understanding of the net that enveloped them.

Nitcheve had killed Ivan, mistaking him for a traitor, but the traitors were not there.

The days of triumph—which is to say, those when the nihilists had appeared in enormous numbers, the trial of the hundred and ninety-three—all appeared to them to be handfuls of sand thrown in the face by the wind.

They too were in those handfuls of sand, in which the torment mingled the epochs; the past of a moment ago and the past of a thousand years ago were confused. The individuals lashed by the tempest seemed to be atoms, glowing in the radiance of the idea.

Sexes and ages also seemed to be mingled in these giant struggles; the children, the old, women: Juvenelienne, Sweskow, Sophia Perovskaya, the hundred and eight-six students of St. Petersburg, the Herculean Rogatchev, Kovalik, the president of an instruction-room, with his wife, Mikhailov and the others![40]

How many phantoms! Phantoms too, they were about to be less even than phantoms.

The procession arrived at Horseguards Square.

On one side was the cloister; on the other, the gallows.

A hundred thousand spectators were watching, all eyes.

The crow perched on the gallows flew away, uttering a loud screech. Perching on the branch of a tree, it waited.

The first of the condemned went up to the platform, looked at the crowd, in which he recognized his friend

---

[40] Only the names I have amended as Perovskaya and Mikhailov correspond to those of well-known *narodniki*.

and his fiancée. This was their wedding; a red wedding, as ever.

There was not a tremor in the face of the condemned man, nor on those of his companions, and especially not on the face of his fiancée. They had been seen; was that not sufficient? Another, a widow, had her children in her arms in order that their father could see them with his final gaze.

The executioner put the black bag over the head of the first, adjusted the rope, and released the platform. Then it was the turn of the second.

When the three black bags were hanging at the ends of the ropes, like enormous fruit, the crowd slowly flowed away, and then the soldiers, also slowly. Then the crow came back, and others with it. Alexandra and the mother with her sons watched for a long time.

Subterranean paths do not only exist in St. Petersburg, and from city to city, the hunters and the hunted often cross paths underground.

XXVII. The Lake

The regular pruning of the human hedge by war is known, after Machiavelli, as "the reason of State." He cites others too; there are numerous reasons of state of the same kind—such as the reason of state that has some dove brooding on its nest killed by falcons.

Thus are artists born of dynasties of kings.

Three young men, all artists, being born with the same sensitive delicate and intelligent nature, their nerves strung like harps, their brains haunted by grandiose dreams, their hearts full of love, encountered one another.

They had the same constitution, the same tastes and, strangely enough, the same face.

Perhaps they shared the same ancestor, perhaps it was due to an identical combination of circumstances.

They were united by a great friendship.

They were almost the same age. Jacques and Hermann were artists; Ludwig was a monarch by profession—which is to say, a monarch by title, because he was an artist, like the other two.[41]

For the unfortunates riveted to the chains of their ancestors, ministers governed. The people paid, bled dry, while waiting for a heart; they paid for the ministers' expenses and the king's love of music.

---

[41] Following standard French literary practice, the author renders the third name as "Louis," but is not trying to conceal the fact that he is referring to Ludwig II of Bavaria (1845-1886), who was deposed by a conspiracy whose means were trumped-up accusations of madness and (probably) murder.

Our three young men lived in harmony. The spectra of colors and the music of the spheres sang in their eyes and ears, and all their senses, charmed, combined with one another, melted into the infinite harmony. The eddies of waves and crowds and the beating of their hearts were all a rhythm.

Separated for a few years by the return of Jacques to his homeland—France—they exchanged frequent correspondence on the subject of their art.

Ludwig's immense theater was nearly finished. Hermann had come to look for Jacques.

In that theater, the forests and lakes were authentic, thunder rumbled, repeated by the echoes of caverns; birds pecked the fruits of service-trees, as red as blood.

The lake, especially—a deep lake fringed with shade by oaks and old willows, whose branches dipped into the water—was charming.

The same evening that Hermann arrived in Paris, both sheltered by the enormous dome of the Salle Gaucher, they talked about the marvelous theater, where nothing more was lacking but the reunion of the three artists, to awaken its magical songs.

Wagner would be performed there as he ought to be. The Valkyrie would have a plain on which to descend, a genuine battlefield where crows would be circling in the air while she offered the brave the cup of the dead. They talked about all that lovingly. They read a few letters, complaining that they were often seized by various dark committees, as if they contained state secrets, and ended up talking bitterly about the police of their own country and others—to which two men of evil appearance sitting at the next table listened attentively.

Those two men, whom we shall call Nicaise and Gasparin, were pretending to read newspapers, in order to listen more closely. Nicaise was holding his upside-down.

Those men were perplexed; the orders they had received were not easy to carry out: to arrest the two young men who had been indicated to them, but to arrest the without the slightest scandal, for some blatant crime, and to do so before midnight that very day.

It was eight o'clock in the evening, so the agents were in a quandary.

The true reason for the arrest was that their correspondence could not be deciphered by the dark committee. It would have been quite simple, but it required a knowledge of various ancient and modern systems of notation. No one thought of that, although it was the most obvious thing in the word that such enthusiastic musicians would write in musical signs—but it is not the custom to see that which leaps to the eyes.

Also, the word Paris in Ludwig's last missive had been represented by two Hindu characters, the *pa* and the *ri*, which correspond to the *mi* and *so* of our notation. Those signs, followed by the Persian word *bilesra* (quickly) plunged a host of men of State into great perplexity.

That manner of correspondence was highly fantastic; it would have caused a sensation at Charenton. The difficulties to which they had been subjected excused that childishness.

It was after that last letter that the arrest warrants had been issued.

"There will be superb brass effects," Herman said to Jacques. "Ludwig studied that in the war of 1870. Certain fields are immense amphitheaters."

With their elbows on the little table, they were dreaming.

Suddenly, the remembered that the principal condition of the journey, money, was lacking. They had notified Ludwig, being unable to stretch to two railway tickets with all their resources combined.

The response ought to have arrived, they thought. It would not be late.

It was, however, to be permanently delayed, because Ludwig had never received their letter.

Then they set about imitating various motifs that they had in their ears as a mariner hears the waves there—fresh and beautiful things, strange things and comical things: the polka of the dark committee, the jig of brass bands, love songs reminiscent of the sound of raindrops, or the songs of nightingales and skylarks, with naïve rhythms, old folk-songs simulating the sound of spinning-wheels, follies and beautiful things, all so well-done that Nicaise and Gasparin shivered in horror.

But to arrest them would have caused a scandal; they needed to catch them committing a crime—and it was already nine o'clock.

Suddenly, the two young men were speaking slowly, another current carrying them away beyond his world.

"Oh," said Herman, "this theater is only the first seed of a sheaf that will grow into a crop."

"Yes," said the other, "if we could hear now the marvelous songs that will be heard in the future, and which, today, would be fatal."

And from the future, by means of powerful wing-beats, they returned to the past, singing the old slave song with the terrible rhythm:

The ax is red with blood,
And red too is the torch

Red is the rising sun,
And redder still it will set.

What blood-drinkers! thought Nicaise and Gasparin, forgetting that an anarchist meeting had begun in the back room. They had seen plenty of them, Nicaise and Gasparin.

Suddenly, songs with a virile rhythm rose up from the next room like gusts of wind:

I have rifles, scythe and picks,
Without the thunder and lightning,
To dispose of the entire clique
Of exploiters of the world.

That one, to the tune of a Breton ballad—and so many, many others.

Then, gripped by the breaths that filled the room, they improvised songs and words at the top of their voices, wholeheartedly:

It's a legend that is rising
Blowing in the clarions of the wind,
Like the waves, like the tide
The masses are rising in oceans.
Like the sea that extends and rumbles,
Humans, black or white,
Will cover the old world!

The crime had been found.

It was not a legend but Gasparin who replied, and politely invited the young men to come into the other room on a matter of business.

Ah! It must be Ludwig's reply. They both hurried.

It was Nicaise who was waiting for them, plastered so tightly against the wall that two idlers at the end of the street were arguing about the genre of painting in relief.

"It's simply distemper," said one.

"Get away—it's a genuine relief, a kind of Chinoiserie with fabric garments.

"I tell you that it's whitewash."

"And I tell you that it's a relief."

"I assure you that it is."

"I assure you that it isn't."

The arrest was easy; they had no suspicion that they were dealing with two agents. Jacques and Hermann gladly marched side by side with them, sometimes preceding them, only regretting one thing—not having a sou to buy a drink for Ludwig II's envoys.

They put on such a good show of guiding the others that when they reached Bureau X of the international police they approached the head of the bureau with such alacrity and in such a manner that he was deceived.

By a singular chance, the head of the Bureau was replacing the true one for a few hours, and was only vaguely familiar with the affair. Holding out the stack of gold coins ready to pay the agents to Herman, he completed the misapprehension.

It was just enough for the journey.

"You can go," he said, in the tone of someone who does not want to be disturbed any longer—and turning to Nicaise and Gasparin, whom he assumed to be prisoners, he added: "And you, Messieurs, sit down here and await my orders."

The surprise was all the more complete because the veritable head of the Bureau was in no hurry to come back. They were in the middle of a political crisis; the orders of the present moment might be dangerous to carry out a little later.

The Bureau was in double disarray; the personnel having been renewed the day before, Nicaise and Gasparin were just as unknown there as their prisoners. Furthermore, the news telegraphed from their country as so terrible that the staff of Bureau X were losing their heads.

Suddenly spotting Nicaise and Gasparin sitting on their bench, and thinking that it was hardly worth the trouble of arresting those young men to treat them so well, the head of the Bureau said to himself: *These fellows certainly have sinister faces; they're doubtless revolutionaries, and prudence is the mother of security.* He had them accompanied into a cell that opened on to the corridor.

With their nervous and sensitive constitution, Herman and Jacques had felt ill at ease in the Bureau; they had left without asking any questions. Did they not know that Ludwig was waiting for them?

Without knowing why, they hastened their departure, going directly from Bureau X to the Gare de l'Est.

Why, they wondered, *did Ludwig employ such strange people to send us the money for the journey?*

"That Bureau is a wolf's mouth."

"After all, perhaps one's safer there."

Once they were on the train they were more tranquil, and did not worry for long about that which was to change their art.

A train during the hours of night is favorable to misty legends. They talked about one of Ludwig's scenarios.

It was said to be based on a true story.

Otto, the hero, has not yet encountered a woman as beautiful as his dream, or as pleasant as the sound of lutes, as pure as he wants his beloved to be.

He meets a beautiful woman with golden hair and flesh impregnated with light; she is the one he loves in his heart.

The young woman listens to him meekly. Together, they climb into a boat on a dark lake shaded by tall oaks and willows whose branches dip into the water.

Otto plies the oars in silence, because words, he thinks, cannot express what he is feeling.

Suddenly, he raises his head; the infinite harmony singing with him, he does not look at her with his eyes, from which tears of happiness are escaping; he sees her with his heart.

The young woman is also silent.

The sky is red; it is dawn. Otto does not know whether he has crossed the black wave of life in that boat, whether he is already dead, and whether, in order to live, he ought to disembark from the boat in which the golden-haired maiden is sitting.

He sings; his voice is more beautiful than any human voice; then he falls silent again, not knowing whether he will ever speak.

Then, opening her rosy lips, she pronounces in a hoarse voice the words of a streetwalker.

Horror grips Otto: a horror as infinite as his love was.

Everything crumbles; the stars go out in the sky; there is chaos; there is death.

Then he seizes the specter of his love by her golden hair and hurls her into the lake.

The legend was true; the woman had been saved by those who has sent her to him—courtiers whose orders she had followed.

When Jacques and Hermann arrived the city was full of crowds; the knell was keening in the air; monks in black hoods, such as one saw in days of old were preceding a coffin laden with flowers, which was followed by an army.

Brass instruments filled the air with their sharp notes; muffled drums resonated as if underwater.

They learned that Ludwig was dead.

In Hermann's house, where he lived with his mother, a letter was waiting.

I feel as healthy, physically and morally, as any king, and the treason plotted against me is so surprising that I do not even have time to take measures against the criminal attempts to murder me.

My brave and faithful friends will not abandon me, and if they are prevented by violence from safeguarding my rights, this proclamation and my appeal will be heard by all.

Copies of that letter were sent to all the king's friends—but heard by none. Apart from the peasants whose hearts remain young, no one paid any attention to it; they thought he was mad.

So much blood had been sweated for his theaters and other fantasies, that those who paid eternally were weary.

Hermann and Jacques did not have time to reflect upon the situation; a squad was waiting for them at the door.

"Was it you who were corresponding with Ludwig?"

"Yes, it was us."

"Come with us."

They were taken to the bureau of the international police corresponding with Bureau X in Paris, from which the warrant had been sent.

A summary interrogation took place at the bureau, after which the two friends were separated.

Hermann was brought in first.

"You admit having corresponded with the late king?"

"Of course."

"Read this to me."

With a tragic gesture, the chief of police lifted a packet of letters in his red and greasy hands, as if it were a trophy taken from the enemy.

By chance, Hermann put his hand in his pocket to take out his handkerchief. There was a movement of recoil throughout the bureau, and the chief grabbed the revolver that as set before him, but the fear dissipated.

Two of the incriminating letters were handed to Hermann, which he read without hesitation; there was mention therein of an opera in which a minister is killed by the king he has betrayed.

All that must have contained terrible hidden meanings; the revolutionaries must have profited from the king's madness to acquire state secrets.

That universal revolution in art was doubtless the Red Internationale.

When the reading had concluded, the chief of the bureau spread out all the correspondence on the table. "Will you please explain to me the signs contained in these letters," he said.

"First, I need to give you some explanations regarding various musical notations," Hermann replied, seriously.

The chief of police got up. "Take the gentleman to cell 27," he said.

The agents took Hermann out through one of the doors opening into the office.

Jacques, introduced in his turn, was obliged to read the same letter.

The chief of police saw a double meaning there; his mind refused to believe that anyone was not lying. "What is the significance," he demanded, "of this sequence of letters scattered at the top of the page?"

"It's a fugue written in the German notation. Don't you know the scale?" And mechanically, he began to sing: "C D E F G..."

He did not have time to go any higher; the G remained in his throat.

Were all the madmen in Europe going to be their envoys? The policeman marched up and down with long strides, making furious gestures.

Jacques, for his part, wondered if they had been dealing with madmen for the last two days. Perfectly calm, he looked at the chief of police.

A complication cropped up. Jacques was French; the warrant did not say what had to be done with him.

A compromise got him out of the affair.

The prison hospital is not for dogs; it was there that Jacques was transferred, into the section for furious lunatics.

From the Isar, gently curved in an arc, watercourses branch like broken twigs.

Beside the railway station to the east, the river slows down, bearing a long island full of barracks. Skirting two cemeteries, other watercourses join it upstream, forming an island shaped like a willow-leaf.

From the armored vehicle, a form of transport used by all governments, Jacques saw all that through a hole in the wall—and also the palace gardens where the theater was.

His calmness surprised the director of the hospital, but lunatics are deceptive. The director shivered, seeing that they had forgotten to tie up the madman. What imprudence! That calm, if it was not a ruse or the beginning of a healing process, might presage a fit of furious delirium.

Once in the cell he was left alone.

Jacques sat down on the bed attached to the wall, and began to reflect.

A torn and crumpled piece of paper that had fallen from the doctor's pocket was lying on the ground. Jacques picked it up.

It was a copy of the notice posted by the police regarding Ludwig's death.

After having obeyed the prescriptions of the medical committee during the day, the King left with his physician to take a walk in the park. Some time having past without the returning, a search was mounted, and they were found drowned in the lake.

Both the King and the physician were still showing feeble signs of life, but all attempts to recall them to life failed. At midnight, the deaths of the King and the physician were certified.

The rest was partly torn, but sinister details of the drama remained.

Ludwig's watch, stopped by the water that had penetrated it, marked six-fifty three. It was at eleven o'clock that his cadaver and that of the doctor were discovered in the lake. At that spot the water is about one meter fifty deep.

At six-fifteen on the day of his death the doctor had sent a telegram to the president of the council. A few hours later, both were dead. The mud on the edge of the lake had been trampled in a desperate struggle. The doctor's face and that of the King bore traces of profound scratches. Ludwig's footsteps went further than those of the physician; his overcoat was found on the edge of the lake.

The King's brother, who should succeed him, is, it is said afflicted by the same malady...

The fragments stopped there.
It was the end of their beautiful dream.

XXXVIII. The Lady of the Lake

A certain archbishop *in partibus*, temporarily resident in the city of X***, also loved music.

Between two chalices and several cups of Rhenish wine, he had the scores of Wagner performed, just like Ludwig.

There was an ear to modern passions in that music; that is why it pleased the Walloon Archbishop. His friend, the director of the hospital, often attended soirées hosted by the archbishop in his seminary in Munster, perhaps preferring the prologue to the soirée—which is to say, the dinner—but did not detest hearing the maestro's masterpieces.

One day, he wanted to regale the archbishop in his turn by bringing him a madman full of talent—enlightened by his care, and already partly cured—who sang *Lohengrin* in a remarkable fashion.

The archbishop was delighted, and, the legend of the Holy Grail being all that exists of the most divine, resolved to have the piece performed in his chapel, such a voice not being encountered often.

After Vespers the following Sunday, Jacques, brought by the director, sang in the midst of a profound silence.

There was a deluge of tears; if anyone had dared, there would have been a deluge of flowers.

A richly-dressed lady, her golden hair spilling out from her veil, prostrated herself on the paving-stones, sobbing.

The chief of Bureau X, in sending Jacques to the prison infirmary, had only mentioned dementia. Jacques was absolutely calm, thanks to the savant alienist who had cared for him. After that proof, there was no reason for the madman to be set at liberty; the case had not been serious—although it is true that slightness often counts for nothing in those sorts of things.

The adventure slowly divulged the mystery that enveloped the correspondence of the three artists, which was not well-known. Jacques was surprised to receive mercy.

One of the youngest among the Men of State having suggested that the correspondence of a madman and two performers was not to be dreaded, people turned their back on him with profound pity.

The chief of Bureau X, intent on repairing the error he had made in only mentioning Jacques' madness, thought night and day about finding the key to the correspondence, and finally thought that he had it.

It was not within the walls of his cell that Jacques would talk.

No man would ever discover the secret of the famous symbols; it was therefore necessary to employ a woman. They knew one of them who had no peer for such a task; it was true that she had once been thrown in the water, but that was by a madman. She now had thoroughly proven experience.

She had squandered many fortunes and poured many secrets into the ear of her protector, the chief of Bureau X. She would serve him again on this occasion, the beautiful Georgine, with the figure of a divinity and the voice of a crow. Brandy had left its croak and its fumes in that charming throat.

Jacques was permitted to take long walks in the enclosed gardens of the castle. These gardens were the same ones where the theater was, with its lake shaded by tall oaks. There, as if by chance, he saw a tall woman pass by silently, her golden hair hanging loose—perhaps a prisoner like himself.

But what was the point of talking to her? She must be a prisoner like him. From opposite sides of the shore they saw one another pass by; that was all.

That situation might have lasted a long time, inasmuch as Georgine was playing the same role that she had played with Ludwig, the madman at whose head she had been thrown, rather poorly.

Memories rose up from the heart, and in the solitude, the fresh odor of the water drowned her heart; she had been sad for a long time, searching the theaters and churches for an accent similar to the voice she had once heard.

That accent she had found on the evening when Jacques sang to the Muses.

Something told her that she would find it again.

She was weary of the life she led; was it her fault if she had been plucked too green, as one picks fruit in spring? Afterwards, how could she have left the route that had been mapped out for her in her shame?

Today, something good was coming back to her; the beautiful fruit picked while green was trying to ripen without sunlight.

How many there are like that!

In her early childhood, she had been doomed; as a young woman she had committed an infanticide, of which her mother had been accused in her stead without saving her. She had fled to Bavaria, where the courtiers had made her what she was. Her mother was still searching for her; she was Reine Félix.

One evening, in the park, Georgine found herself face to face with Jacques.

The chief of Bureau X had made horrible threats against her. She was, therefore, good for nothing—what use were the large sums that she was paid?

She never succeeded in anything when it came to important things. It was time to try something else.

Her meeting with Jacques gave her the idea of putting an end to it, but not in the manner desired by the police.

The opportunity presented itself; who could tell whether she would ever find another?

She dared not speak, knowing the effect of her voice. She beckoned to Jacques.

He remembered the scenario sketched by Ludwig, the legend of Otto. Was this, then, the lady of the lake, who had come back?

It was indeed.

Georgine sat down at the foot of a willow, whose branches curved over her.

Then, amid all the horrors spread around them, beside the softly palpitating lake, they made love.

Only one thing was greater than the fatality that enveloped them, and that was death.

Like the swan-knight, Jacques had dreamed of love. This, then, was the one he ought to love.

Georgine had the terrible beauty of Elsa, but there was horror mingled with it.

She told him everything! Everything, in her hoarse voice, her terrified voice.

But who, then, commences in the branches that faint chorus whose pianissimo resembles the drops of water that a storm sheds on the leaves?

Now the storm bursts, terribly; it takes them, envelopes them; they are storm themselves; they make love in the unchained elements.

There is a boat moored to the willows. Jacques unties it, takes up the oars and gently strokes the water of the lake. He sings, as Ludwig had sung, the refrains of *Lohengrin*, and then those that are floating in the air, and in the icy waters of the lake.

The storm rages, then, just as, after the curse, in Wagner's work a terrible silence falls.

Georgine, standing in the bow of the boat, is lit up by the lightning.

Then, there is nothing but darkness, ripped apart by the lightning; the tempest covers them with night; one enormous thunderclap, and the boat turns over; they are plunged into the water.

The death would have been beautiful; the woman had that luck. Jacques did not. They had the cruelty to reanimate him. It was something worse than his body that remained at the bottom of the lake it was his reason.

This time, there was no injustice in putting the musician in the hospital for the insane.

At first, his ideas floated like the mist; his brain tried to retain them by an instinctive effort, similar to the one that attracts parcels of astral matter toward the center around which they rotate.

The sensation that he experienced broke both his head and his heart. The poor fellow lived in that turbulence, trying to get a grip on himself again, but could not do it. A time came when he stopped trying. His nerves vibrating at hazard within his broken-down organism, he established a kind of false equilibrium, like the Leaning Tower of Pisa.

As one becomes thirsty without thinking about it, he had an unconscious desire to see the lady of the lake again, to feel once again the immense joy and immense suffering that he had experienced face to face with her in the boat.

Toward that fugitive image he directed his voice, the only strength that he had conserved intact, but which took on terrible tones.

People came to stand beneath the windows of the madhouse in order to listen, with terror and delight, to the frightful manifestations of that harmonic power, which sometimes took flight with great wing-beats and departed, further and further, all his vigor driving it in that direction.

Only his ears lived an immense life in which, by virtue of that reason alone, everything had taken refuge.

That lasted for several months. Then, because of its very acuity, that morbid state began to calm down.

He remained a brute, a human beast capable of all the monstrous disorders in which a human being descends lower than an animal. In that brutalization, his vital faculties had found their equilibrium.

Jacques became calm again, eating, drinking, and maintaining a dismal silence. There was no longer any reason for anyone to pay attention to him.

Everything, except for the appetites that developed increasingly, had sunk in the sinister lake, but above it, memories still hovered like dragonflies.

Then he fades away in a sensation that is always the same; he sees the lake again; the storm has passed; the water is no longer palpitating like a breast; it is as smooth as marble. Drops of water fall from branches.

In time, Hermann's mother had succeeded in understanding the meaning of the correspondence. She had sent it to Ludwig's successor, who, by chance, the letter reached. Also by chance, an order was issued to set Hermann free. He had been confused with someone else:

a shady financier named Ulric Hermann. It was for that reason that the king's proposal was greeted by his councilors with that success. They thought they were setting the financier free, but set free the artist.

Jacques, for his part, was no longer giving any sign of madness. He was set free too.

XXXIX. One for the Other

For a long time, the financier Hermann had been waiting for the pardon that he had immediately demanded.

How could they let him languish for so long? We know—it was because there had been an error. Hermann the musician had been released instead of Hermann the capitalist.

Madame Hermann, the capitalist's wife, appeared in her husband's eyes to be the cause of the delay. For once, she was innocent, having no need of her husband's absence to deceive him.

This is how the financier Hermann had come to be imprisoned—which is to say, this is the accusation brought against him. As usual, he had not done what he was accused of doing; he had done something else.

Ulric Hermann, well-endowed by nature—handsome, with a frank expression, a prompt intelligence that was once noble—had changed a great deal. He had had a big heart too, which a generous blood had caused to beat. Now his heart was as hard as metal, his blood icy, his intelligence perfidious.

His brother, Hans Hermann, and he were well liked. They had worked for a long time, supporting one another in their studies; then, being the sons of a financier, they had both engaged in speculation. They had ventured into the pestiferous regions where the plague and fever of gold are endemic.

Can one breathe crime perpetually without becoming criminal, or going mad?

At first, the profit of one did not seem harmful to the profit of the other. The two birds of prey from the same nest brought back prey together.

An inheritance from a distant relative, left to Hans, of whom he had been particularly fond, awoke a sentiment of cupidity in the two brothers, satisfied in one and discontented in the other. The thought of taking possession of their common wealth occurred to them both at the same time, developing simultaneously, without anything apparently having changed in their behavior.

A circumstance determined the crime.

Hans was about to marry a young woman whom he loved.

Ulric sensed the river of gold changing its course, to flow into a different ocean.

Sometimes his eyes fixed on Hans with an intensity that caused the latter to shiver, but the preoccupations of his marriage and the joy of his love absorbed him.

Destiny and chance took a hand in the matter. Ulric and Hans encountered one another on a footbridge over a branch of the Isar diverted on to their property for a fabulous price. The thread of water slid through the immense park, a caprice of their childhood in the time when they had used their eyes to admire nature, wanting it for themselves.

Rustically constructed of entwined branches, attached to the banks by the trunks of willows, the footbridge curved in a bold vault over the watercourse, hollowed into a pol. All around was a profound wood; below, the water was black and deep.

On seeing Hans coming, fear seized Ulric's throat; he sensed the crime coming. Would it be his own or his brother's? Ulric, for his part, saw the horizon streaming with gold coming back toward him; the clouds were sparkling with wisps of gold. His brain was red hot, as if it were melting. In the blackness of the lake, the face of a corpse frightened him; it was his own.

Hans was still coming closer; he too had strange thoughts. It seemed to him that Death was driving them toward one another, that he was about to fight with his brother, and that one of the two would not return home.

The footbridge trembled beneath their footfalls. The shadow turns their heads.

Ulric was the first to throw himself upon the other. There was blood in his eyes.

Ulric was the stronger.

Hans' corpse was only found a long time afterwards. Ulric was imprisoned not for the death of his brother, for whom he had ordered assiduous searches everywhere that he was not, but for a financial swindle that, for once, he had not committed.

Ulric went pale when he was arrested. It was, however, with a form voice that he demanded to know of what he was accused. On the specification of the crime, the financier recovered all his arrogance.

Remorse does not come immediately; an action that has just been committed has a numbing effect, and, humans not being designed for crime, a disturbance of the entire being; thoughts are unclear. It is afterwards, on mulling over the details, sometimes insignificant, that the sharp claws of remorse begin to tear at the heart.

Some people never feel that; Ulric might never have done so, incessantly busy with the cares of the administration of his brother's wealth and the searches he organized, but his arrest put an end to all that. Prison gave him time to reflect.

One evening, the governor was introduced into the financier's cell.

Ulric had asked for release over and over. *That*, he thought, *is what he is coming to announce to me.*

"I have," the governor said, "a difficult mission to carry out in your respect."

Ulric recoiled, struck by the ominous quality of that beginning.

"The minute searches you began in the matter of your brother have been continued. Perhaps you retained some vague hope of finding him alive."

"Indeed," said Ulric.

"That hope is about to be destroyed, which I regret profoundly. Your brother has been found in a pond on your property; the cadaver bears the marks of a desperate struggle. Your brother has been murdered."

Ulric thought that he felt the judge's eyes looked into his heart.

The other had no thought of anything but a profound commiseration; suspicion could not rose as high as the financier.

"This dolorous event has caused the realization that the gross error has been committed, to your detriment. You should have been released some time ago, and the ministers had given the order to do so; it has just been realized that another Hermann, a wretched musician, has benefited from the error. Because of the discovery of the corpse of your unfortunate brother, Their Excellencies have ordered your release."

The governor was searching for the most soothing words for that great grief.

Thus the financier Hermann was released. He went to arrange his brother's funeral, and especially to assist in the investigation, for he wanted to find the murderer.

A large number of witnesses who had not seen anything came forward. It was Ulric who was seeking, in advance of the examining magistrate, those who had revelations to make. A few eventually turned up who were so important that he had some desire to get rid of such inconvenient witnesses. He even tried to do so.

For example, a young girl, little Cath, had seen Hans go into the great park of their property near the Isar; she had followed him with her eyes as far as the footbridge. "There," she said, "another man, about the same height as you, Monsieur Ulrich, came up to him. It was about eight o'clock in the evening; the moon was shining on the water. I saw the two men hurl themselves at one another; I was scared. I carried on watching, but the night had become too dark."

"What is your address, my dear child," said Ulric.

Cath gave her address.

Ulric was perplexed. For him, there was no doubt that the girl could doom him by repeating innocently to the judges, as she had just done to him, what she had seen. If he enjoined her to keep silent, he was still doomed; only death could render her mute without accusing him.

He no longer regarded a human life in the same light. Once a change has taken place, one does not return to one's original state. The decision was rapidly made.

Ulric carefully inscribed the girl's name on a separate page of his notebook. The page, like the girl's life, would be thrown to the wind.

"I need," he said, "the names and addressed of the people to whom you have confided this testimony. You understand how large the reward will be for those who help me to avenge my brother."

"My father, my mother and my sister are the only ones I've told."

"What does your father do?"

"He's a blacksmith, near the bridge in your garden."

"You may be sure that he'll no longer have any need to work now."

The little girl had large tears in her eyes; it broke her heart that they would owe their good fortune to man's death.

"That virtuous impulse honors you, child," said Ulric. "For now, you're going to complete your deposition in the same place, so that I can make sure that your imagination hasn't deceived you. Come with me."

Night was falling, as on the day when Cath Edmond had seen the crime.

A few frissons, of fear or memory, or perhaps the cool of the evening, passed through her. They had left the house by a hidden door, but she thought nothing of that.

Following the paths through the wood, broad at first and then narrower, they arrived at the footbridge.

"It was just here, wasn't it?" said Ulrich, making her go ahead of him.

"Yes," said Cath, who was trembling, hearing the heavy footsteps of the murderer behind her, perhaps sensing the magnetic impression of the steel blade he had taken out in order to strike her.

She turned round. Ulric's eyes were shining like embers in his lived face. Then he grabbed her and stabbed her with his dagger—but she, like a stinging bee, bit his cheek when he lowered his face over her, and swiftly threw herself in the pool, which ought to take her outside by way of the stream of the Isar. The little girl knew how to swim.

Ulric raised his hand to his bloody jaw; the wound would be visible for a long time; it was as deep as if it had been made by the teeth of a young dog.

Henceforth, he would have the sword of Damocles over his head, unless he put a end to that family. That was what he planned to do.

A perpetual hunt passes over the earth; some are prey, the others hounds or hunters.

Cath and her family were henceforth among the hunted, but sometimes the game gathers together and stands up to the dogs and hunters.

The young girl told her father what had happened; the workman understood that the life of his child was henceforth in peril. The family left the country. That departure made Ulric anxious.

XI. Patter

"Gather round, ladies and gentlemen. Get as close as you like to the panther's cage and Madame the Somnambulist's consultation-booth. Gather round, ladies and gentlemen; there's still room in the wings for the cripples. Gather round, ladies and gentlemen—squeeze up, gentlemen, to make more room for the ladies. This is the greatest show on earth; here one can hear all the beasts in the menagerie growling, as in the African forest.

"Over there is the ice-cream seller, which reminds one of Mont Blanc, next to the narrow grille with the little holes, to prevent anything passing through—that's the great sea-serpent.

"Here, it's as if one were on a voyage, as if one possessed the land and the sea and the air as well, since this thread is the rope of a captive balloon.

"Go on, ladies and gentlemen, gather together to enjoy what there is to be seen on every side, and to purchase my merchandise.

"Gather round, ladies and gentlemen; if I mention merchandise to you, it isn't what's usually meant by that coarse word, which one assimilates to the thing of Cambronne,[42] but a host of marvels that you're about to see.

"Gather round, ladies and gentlemen; here's powder for dyeing hair brown, blonde or black; one for whitening the teeth and cleaning the fingernails; it makes them pearly and puts a shine on them. Gather round, ladies and gentlemen, it costs two sous. The Shah of Persia

---

[42] i.e., *merde* [shit].

bought two bottles from me for his chamberlain. They're also good in liquor; Queen Victoria puts all of them into her whisky every day.

"Gather round, ladies and gentlemen, listen to that pretty sound; one might think it was castanets, but it's the boxes of the cripples waltzing elegantly in front the Petroff Theater. It's the Russki Ivane whose causing a sensation; only eight years old and dances like a zephyr—not with his legs of course.

"Gather round, ladies and gentlemen, here's the elixir of long life and the elixir of inheritance, each as effective as the other, for two sous. Here's a powder that kills fleas and lice—not that I think you have any, but one can make a gift of it for two sous to those who are afflicted.

"Gather round, ladies and gentlemen, a little courage in the pocket. This is the microscope of the King of Madagascar, made with the ashes of marine plants reduced to glass by fusion; every one of you can do as much with the recipe that accompanies it—ten francs. It's the foundation-stone of my treasures.

"Gather round, ladies and gentlemen..."

But the heat of the day was so overwhelming, such large drops of water were falling from the stormy clouds, that everyone deserted places open to the sky and took refuge in the booths of the fortune-tellers and animal-tamers. The cripples' tent was packed.

There were four children there, between eight and twelve years old, as blond as the Hospodar Lioudoëke and his wife, whom one might take for their parents. The fact is that they were from the same country—the country where people are blond, with steel-gray eyes. They came from Russia.[43]

The young hawker Stéphane, weary of producing his own patter, got down from the table where he was shouting, his box of trinkets in his hands, closed that treasure-trove firmly, took a piece of bread from his pocket and went to eat it in the shelter of the cripples' tent, which was mounted on trestles.

Hospodar Lioudoëke, and especially his wife, did not exactly have a reputation for benevolence. The young salesman Stéphane, instead of soliciting a hospitable shelter under their tent while the rain was falling, simply hid himself behind a heap of various objects used in performances: an empty barrel made him a booth; he was at home there—better than that. Doubling the pleasure of eating his bread to the sound of the storm, from there he could hear what the four little cripples were saying, who had just been brought to have their meal, arranged in a line on a plank serving as a stage, like the beggars they were.

It must be funny, Stéphane thought, *to put their children on the stage every evening to sleep—saves on beds, mind!*

The two impresarios having left, the children, after a moment's silence, began to talk in whispers, so quietly that it was almost a breath—but Stéphane was so close that he could hear them distinctly. It was the youngest one, little Ivane, who began:

"Lèfe, my legs really hurt."

---

[43] The title Hospodar, or Gospodar, is actually Rumanian, and means "Lord." The reason for its application to these two rogues is unclear.

"So much the better! It's because they're still alive. Shut up!"

Another voice replied: "Me too, Lèfe; my knees hurt a lot."

"That's because they can unbend. Shut up!"

Lioudoëka came down, carrying a pile of cups and a bottle of coffee mixed with rum. She gave each child a little coffee and a piece of bread, then went back up.

"*Etote vetchere!*" said the deeper voice of Lèfe, so quietly that Stéphane barely heard it.

The young hawker realized that he had stumbled on a drama. The custom he had of chatting with his comrades of all nations and hearing them talk had taught him a little of every language. He understood Russian as well as French, other children, like him expressed, themselves indifferently in each of the idioms they barely understood.

Now he is mixed up in the poor mites' escape—for he is certainly going to help them. How are the poor kids going to get away, with their limbs having been twisted for such a long time? Fortunately, he has overheard them.

He won't say anything to them; they'd be suspicious. He'll find himself in their path, as if by chance. He's as free as the air, having nothing but his box to tote around the world.

He'll stay awake all night—which is to say, the few hours before dawn. People sleep late in fairgrounds, and this passes for a fairground at Bercy, about three years after the triple execution in St. Petersburg. There have been similar sunrises since, and the gallows has borne more fruit in the meantime.

Little Ivane, entrusted to friends, was the child for whom Alexia, the wife of the hero who died for liberty, was still searching, the man to whom he had entrusted her in the days of peril having disappeared with her.

He had disappeared for the very simple reason that he had been murdered.

Those who had committed the crime, Hospodar Lioudoëke and his wife, then innkeepers on an isolated road on the great steppes, thought the child too young to remember, had kept him for their own use. He remembered, though.

One day, Lioudoëke and Lioudoëka left the inn, no more was hard of them. The inn had been sold to a muzjik, who thought that he would do good business there. He did, but a bad smell coming from his cellar attracted the attention of the police, and a search led to the discovery of putrefying bodies. It was there that Lioudoëke and Lioudoëka had buried the last travelers they had murdered. It was all the same to them, since they were far away.

In consequence of that discovery the muzjik was hanged. Lioudoëke and Lioudoëka were rolling peacefully around the world.

Perhaps, according to the idea they had of the law, they had done it with that intention.

In addition to little Ivane, of whom they tried to make a monster, the Lioudoëkes stole other children. It was safer than buying them, they told themselves; one need not fear anyone's testimony. Thus, they acquired Anna's sons, the sons of the judge Philippe; they were so prudent that anyone who cast an inquisitive glance at their way of life had never emerged from their hostelry.

In spite of all his prudence, Lioudoëke was deceived by a child during the sixth month of his journey; he was not to see him again for three years.

As he was able to buy ready-made monsters for his human menagerie without compromising himself, he made a deal with another showman for a cripple the latter had "prepared," by tying up his legs, loosely at first and then increasingly tightly, until the folded limbs, put in a box, no longer obtained any nourishment and atrophied completely.

The child bought by Lioudoëke was about twelve years old. His resolution was remarkable; in the same way that he emerged from the box and trailed his deformed legs every time he could escape surveillance, he made the other poor unfortunates do the same.

While Lioudoëke and his wife were sleeping heavily, when they had drunk to much alcohol, Lèfe and his little comrades in misfortune emerged from their boxes, arranged like the pots in which geese are imprisoned to make their livers swell, dragging themselves around like crabs—their bodies enlarged in spite of their poor nourishment—trying to support themselves on their twisted and tremulous legs. Sometimes they succeeded.

The moment came when Lèfe talked about escape.

Trembling and charmed, they agreed; then the day was fixed.

What a mirage of happiness, and what fear!

Stéphane, having wondered for some time how he could help the poor kids, told himself that it was better to wait for circumstances to develop. His plan could not fail, since he did not have one, and chance would eventually furnish him with something to follow or avoid; that would help him.

What an adventure!

The first inspiration was to make use of the drunkenness of the Lioudoëkes to put them to sleep. He even regretted not having among his famous powders anything that had any other virtue than the power of suggestion.

Stéphane had an idea. He covered his head and ran to the booth of his comrade the tooth-puller.

"Hey, Canicule!" No one knew why the young man's name, which was Canis, had been made into Canicule—perhaps by contrast, Canis being rather chilly.[44]

"What is it?" he said, half asleep.

"Give me something for my toothache."

"Would you like me to pull them out?"

"Certainly not! I want some drug to put me to sleep."

"It's not worth the trouble of me getting up, then. Lift the latch of the booth and take what you want; there's laudanum in the red glass bottle—that gives it a ruby tint, you know."

"Good—I've got it. Thanks."

"Don't take too much—it'll give you a bad turn."

"Don't worry."

"Goodnight—close the latch again; animals sometimes escape. Brutus took to his heels yesterday like a cat."

"It's closed."

Stéphane had a substantial supply of laudanum. That's good, he said to himself. With two nice glasses of absinthe to dilute it, the Lioudoëkes will sleep like logs.

As he passed in front of the cripples' tent, Stéphane simulated a fall, dragging with him a piece of wood, which made a noise on the stairs of their den. The two spouses came out.

---

[44] This is presumably a joke, but its import is unclear.

"What's that you're demolishing, you filthy *vrodiaga*?" *Vrodiaga* meant vagabond; he was accustomed mix languages when he swore.

"Don't get annoyed. I tripped. My toothache is preventing me from seeing clearly.

Then seeing a bottle shining in the young man's pocket: "You didn't break your brandy?"

"No. At your service if you want to have a drink with me."

"Come in!"

Now they're all sitting down, with three full glasses, drinking together.

The Lioudoëkes start drinking; Stéphane moistens his lips in his glass and puts his hands to his cheeks, crying out in pain: "Oh, my teeth! My teeth!" And he runs out.

"We'll have the lion's share of it," say the two drunks, stupidly caught in the trap, sharing out the third glass.

This time they sleep until mid-morning without getting undressed, with no other bed but the planks of the tent.

They were in that state of lethargy when Stéphane went into the cripples' store-room at about three o'clock in the morning, having heard them wriggling around in the dark.

He struck a match, and took account of the scene.

The children, frozen with terror at the sight of him, had suspended their preparations.

"Don't be afraid," he said. "Where are you going?"

"We don't know."

"Well, I know—you're going to come to my house, to the hotel where I rent a room to sleep in when I have the time. The difficulty is getting there. Let's see –you, the eldest, you can see that I'm a friend—Stéphane, the little hawker, you know."

"That's true," said Lèfe. "We believe you."

"How do you get out of here?"

"They showed him a hole in the floor, contrived with great difficulty.

"Can you walk?"

"Yes!"

It could not really be called walking; if it had been daylight, the escape would have been impossible.

"Lèfe, take Ivane. I'll take care of the other two. You're brave, Lèfe; walk, since you want to be free."

The entire fairground was asleep; only the roar of an angry tiger and the yawning of a bored lion were audible in the cool air that precedes the dawn.

From the fairground a Bercy to what Stéphane called his "hotel"—the *Rabid Dog*, near the Place Maube—it was a long way, but, not having the time to be scared, the children had at least two chances in a thousand of getting there.

They've got a funny way of getting about, Stéphane said to himself, gazing at Lèfe and Ivane, who were trying to get the numbness out of their legs, hopping like toads. The other two were even worse; it was better to carry them. It was Stéphane who sweated under the burden.

"A lovely family!" said an early-rising market-gardener, looking at them in amazement. "I regret not seeing the female who produced those monsters!"

Stéphane, the sweat running down his face, was walking ever more rapidly. Lèfe was following him, dragging Ivane as best he could, when, suddenly stifled by the race and the open air, the latter two fell in a faint.

As often happens, that which ought to have doomed them saved them.

A drunken man going along the Quai de la Rapée, led by his horse, approached the group.

"Why, it's the little street-hawker Stéphane. What are you doing with this brood of brats?"

"They're my little brothers, who've arrived by train from Lyon; they're used to the country, and the bad air of Paris has got to them-their lungs and their legs have given way—look at them."

"Put them in my cart. Where are you going?"

"Home, to the *Rabid Dog* in the Mouffetard quarter."

"I've finished the work I had to do, and I'm tired. Load them up and lead on. I'm going to sleep."

Père André, red all the way to the ears and extremely weary, climbed up as best he could into the cart and went to sleep.

It was only a matter of piling the silent children in with him, and the two invalids, a trifle less breathless, and then trotting steadily as far as Stéphane's refuge— the safest place, since it was the most obvious. It is always necessary to hide people or things in places too exposed for anyone to bother looking there.

Stéphane arrived at his hotel with such a loud clatter of wheels and hooves that the children in the street got up from the mud where they had sat down to play, perhaps having the delicate intention of patching the backsides of their trousers with that daub, and ran after the carriage all the way to the *Rabid Dog*.

Leaving the man to sleep in comfort, Stéphane got the children inside cleverly enough to conceal their gait.

His bed was in a room with a dozen others.

"Quickly," he said, "Slip into the bed, two at the head. I'm going to get you something to eat. Sleep while you wait."

He gave them that instruction because they were exhausted by the journey. He paid for the food and then returned swiftly to the fairground, taking Père André, who was scarcely awake.

The fellow lived at the end of the Rue de Bercy, in a small hut made of wood, surrounded by rabbit-hutches.

"Madame André!" Stéphane shouted, "I've brought back your man. He's been helping me bring my little brothers from the railway station."

The drunkard confirmed it. Stéphane had four little brothers; he had seen them get off the train. Little Stéphane had taken account of the value of witnesses.

He only just had time to get the stool that served him as a podium and recommence the previous day's patter for the rare passers-by when he got back to the fairground. He was full of zest, young Stéphane, and was even more so when she saw the Lioudoëkes rubbing their eyes at ten o'clock in the morning when they opened their caravan; they had slept exceedingly well.

Stéphane, amused by the dazed demeanor of the two monsters, started singing his patter loud and clear, like a young cockerel, following the tempo of a group of idlers who were singing the fashionable ditty "On the Way Home from the Revue"

I've been on the road forever,
I'm the little street-trader,
With liberty for a comrade.
I'll carry my little gewgaws
The sky above my ceiling.
Come forward, my ladies

255

To listen to my patter.
On its wings, the wind,
Carries far and away
All the words that fall,
Like leaves in a torrent.
Patter, gentlemen,
Is just like a tenant.
Come forward ladies,
You only pay when you buy.

Here is, for sale,
Anything at all.
The world entire,
In this basket
For a banquet
Turn bread to crumbs
To earn my living,
I've a sumptuous feast.

Come closer, here's the magic brew
That will rejuvenate beauty;
It's the iris of the ravine
Distilled in the summer sun.
Here are powders of heritage,
Against fleas and rabies,
And powdered diamond,
With only germinates if sown.
The kings of the Orient
Buy from me often,
Come forward, ladies,
You only pay when you buy.

The cheerful Stéphane only just had time to finish his refrain when he was interrupted by the furious cries of the Lioudoëkes.

"Where are the cripples?"

"Someone's stolen the cripples."

Stéphane went over to the caravan.

"What's happened, respectable Hospodar?"

"Who's stolen them from me!" cried the hoarse voice of Lioudoëke and the shrill voice of Lioudoëka—so sharp and harsh that it pierced the ears like a wound—in chorus.

"It must have been the thief I saw passing by this morning."

"Where was that?"

"He was heading toward the countryside."

"What did he look like?"

"I didn't see the man—I saw a big black vehicle, a little longer than yours."

"I'll take this to law—you'll be a witness."

But Lioudoëke could not appeal to the law; he was afraid that someone might ask him where he got the children. Perhaps they would not have asked him, but all in all, he preferred to keep quiet. One thing made him anxious: once, near his tent, he had seen a tall blonde woman who was looking at two of his prisoners.

She had, indeed, been looking at them, but she was not the one who had taken them.

In the next volume, we shall find once again the ogre Lioudoëke, his wife Lioudoëka, and their victims, the son of the man hanged in Russia and the sons of the judge Philippe Wolff.

Epilogue

The creatures that wallow in the end of our epoch beneath the pale sun of the centuries-long winter, before the new dawn, are being transformed more rapidly as environments are becoming increasingly diversified.

The collapse is mingled everywhere with the emergence.

Some, in that torment, almost possess the humanity that is about to be born; that which was false and atrophied in their development is taking flight, straightening up and moving, warmed by the rising sap.

All the human waves are breaking over old reefs; the death-throes are mingled with the birth.

Gaël, especially, was making rapid progress; his mind ahead of his time, his body bathed by magnetic effluvia, he was becoming young again. It was a strange youth, impregnated with electricity, the molecules of his being renewing themselves, gradually being replaced by others more delicate, saturated with life and light.

His hair, which had become black again, had a phosphorescence in the darkness, and his fingers sometimes emitted a gleam similar to the pallor of moonlight. Sparks sprang from his being; there was no reason why Gaël should die before the end of the world.

Events were moving in great tides, rising as high as they retreated, as they advanced over the banks. But tempests put wind in sails; the landing was imminent.

Nothing astonished Gaël, neither the despair of those who were sick with disgust, nor the cries of the human crows circling over the charnel-houses of war.

The hot revolts of crowds and the cold slaughter of rapacity left him impassive.

On the earth, often washed by the crimson dew of blood, human groups were beginning to gravitate, following the law of universal attraction. Nature, long fought, was taking on a rhythmic march; spheres of evolution were becoming increasingly rapid.

Sometimes, scenes from the past reappeared.

One of the most savage had taken place at the death of one of the women who, in those last times, had not left the furnace, searching for her lost children.

One evening, she recognized them, disfigured, and as she lost consciousness, a group of children started throwing stones at her; one of them struck her on the temple.

"She's drunk!" someone said.

She was dead.

Over her grave, where a few people had saluted the future, hatreds had descended. It was natural, the dead person being a woman, that she was charged with more monstrosities than could have been perpetrated in ten thousand lives. Then the rumor died down; other prey was being chased.

Anna was at peace: being unable to recover her children, she had devoted herself to the revolutionary idea.

One evening, Gaël was walking in the open fields, thinking about the terrestrial tides in which the sun was breathing more and more rapidly, a respiration like that of human breasts. He had an observatory somewhere, in which, through telescopes of enormous power, he watched the sun crusting over with continents, while the earth was laboring in childbirth, and, like everything in nature, from plants running to seed and animals building their nests, humankind was completing its cycle. Having reached the age of virility, it was building the nest of the future.

Thus thought Gaël, while the lights of Paris scintillated in the distance, like constellations, or glow-worms in the grass.

Suddenly, a nearer light attracted his attention.

In the sleeping landscape, a villa was lit up, mysteriously. The filtered light fringed a façade that was evidently veiled; prudent hands had closed the shutters in order to minimize the glare.

A sound of jaws close at hand attracted his attention. Gaël heard furious growling, mingled with the grating sounds that starving animals make as they gnaw bones. He lighted the hooded lantern that he usually carried during his nocturnal peregrinations.

Two exceedingly thin dogs were fighting over human debris that they had stolen somewhere.

There seemed to him to be some connection between that incident and the veiled light of the villa. Calmly, as he watched the human insects performing their dramas, Gaël approached the villa.

The dogs must have got in through a fairly large hole made in the hedge surrounding it. He crawled through it, clutching the lantern to his breast. He arrived beneath the luminous fringe that filtered through three widows with closed shutters. They were on the first floor, but a tangle of ivy and rose-bushes rose up all over the façade. Gaël climbed it with the agility of a cat.

Between the cracks of the shutter he saw a dozen men around a table, some old and others young, with the dazed and curious expressions of excited idlers. Two women of the same sort were with them.

All of them, though fully-dressed, had taken off their gloves; that was necessary because they were rooting around in a cadaver, butchered rather than dissected, on the table. There was an acrid odor in the air. The cadaver, stolen from the cemetery the previous night, might have been there for a month; he flesh was blue—but that putrefaction only served to increase the stupid fury of the rummagers. It was a scramble, the cold scramble of delirious curiosity. They had wanted to see whether the cadaver of a revolutionary was made like any other.

Confronted by that scene, Gaël was bitten by remorse; he remembered a woman vivisected; that crime, accomplished for science, had been horrible; he was conscious of that. The scene that he was seeing was not the same.

These various sentiments faded away, stifled by the study of that savagery, caught in the act.

"Where the devil is the left hand?" said a fat bald man with the greasy head.

"I told you that I heard something," retorted a kind of twisted dwarf, dressed like a marionette.

He was afraid as he said it, thinking of things beyond the tomb.

They're dogs, Gaël thought.

"Come on, don't be silly—you've hidden it," said another voice.

It was a woman who had said that, with a ruddy complexion, thick lips, an enormous chin, her hair coarse and black, in a velvet dress garnished with lace—a character from the Stone Age in a Louis XV costume.

A pale student with a girlish face was taking notes. Nothing escaped him: words, gestures, the setting; the cadaver was only commonplace to him; was it not similar to all the other cadavers?

Gaël felt some sympathy for the young man.

"But it's like the others," said a short clean-shaven fellow enveloped in a vast cape. "There's only the head to see."

They had begun with all the rest, except for the head. There were liqueurs there; they were all drinking from time to time.

They took the head and started taking it apart like everything else. The pale young man, who knew dissection, smiled. Gaël liked him more and more.

"We each need a piece!" exclaimed the woman. "We need to search inside."

A colossus took hold of a hatchet and started chopping the corpses up into pieces; then each one made a selection from the heap of human flakes.

At that moment, the branches supporting Gaël broke; he fell noisily.

The fright was general; everyone ran outside, covering their portion of the quarry under their clothing.

The pale young man, calmly wrapping the head in a piece of paper, with green-tinted shreds of flesh, went out with a plaid tread.

Gaël, who had fallen rather fortunately, went back through the hole in the hedge. He understood that the body of the female revolutionary had just been subjected to the supreme insult of unconscious inquisitiveness.

Through the darkness, he distinguished the tall silhouette of the student, and put his hand on the young man's arm.

"Come with me," he said.

The other followed him.

They went to Gaël's observatory.

There, through the monster telescope, the young man saw singular changes taking place on one of the nearer planets.

"What's that?"

"Signals. It's the beginning of the Internationale of worlds."

The young man thought momentarily that he was dealing with a madman, but Gaël, drawing himself up to his full height, said: "Pay attention—we're going to reply."

SF & FANTASY

Henri Allorge. *The Great Cataclysm*
Guy d'Armen. *Doc Ardan: The City of Gold and Lepers*
G.-J. Arnaud. *The Ice Company*
Charles Asselineau. *The Double Life*
Cyprien Bérard. *The Vampire Lord Ruthwen*
Aloysius Bertrand. *Gaspard de la Nuit*
Richard Bessière. *The Gardens of the Apocalypse*
Albert Bleunard. *Ever Smaller*
Félix Bodin. *The Novel of the Future*
Alphonse Brown. *City of Glass*
André Caroff. *The Terror of Madame Atomos; Miss Atomos; The Return of Madame Atomos; The Mistake of Madame Atomos; The Monsters of Madame Atomos*
Félicien Champsaur. *The Human Arrow; Ouha*
Didier de Chousy. *Ignis*
Captain Danrit. *Undersea Odyssey*
C. I. Defontenay. *Star (Psi Cassiopeia)*
Charles Derennes. *The People of the Pole*
Georges Dodds (anthologist). *The Missing Link*
Harry Dickson. *The Heir of Dracula*
Jules Dornay. *Lord Ruthven Begins*
Alfred Driou. *The Adventures of a Parisian Aeronaut*
Sâr Dubnotal *vs. Jack the Ripper*
Alexandre Dumas. *The Return of Lord Ruthven*
Renée Dunan. *Baal*
J.-C. Dunyach. *The Night Orchid; The Thieves of Silence*
Henri Duvernois. *The Man Who Found Himself*
Achille Eyraud. *Voyage to Venus*
Henri Falk. *The Age of Lead*
Paul Féval. *Anne of the Isles; Knightshade; Revenants; Vampire City; The Vampire Countess; The Wandering Jew's Daughter*
Paul Féval, *fils. Felifax, the Tiger-Man*
Charles de Fieux. *Lamékis*
Arnould Galopin. *Doctor Omega; Doctor Omega & The Shadowmen*
G.L. Gick. *Harry Dickson and the Werewolf of Rutherford Grange*
Edmond Haraucourt. *Illusions of Immortality*
Nathalie Henneberg. *The Green Gods*
V. Hugo, P. Foucher & P. Meurice. *The Hunchback of Notre-Dame*
Michel Jeury. *Chronolysis*

Gustave Kahn. *The Tale of Gold and Silence*
Gérard Klein. *The Mote in Time's Eye*
Jean de La Hire. *Enter the Nyctalope; The Nyctalope on Mars; The Nyctalope vs. Lucifer; The Nyctalope Steps In; Night of the Nyctalope*
Etienne-Léon de Lamothe-Langon. *The Virgin Vampire*
André Laurie. *Spiridon*
Gabriel de Lautrec. *The Vengeance of the Oval Portrait*
Alain le Drimeur. *The Future City*
Georges Le Faure & Henri de Graffigny. *The Extraordinary Adventures of a Russian Scientist Across the Solar System* (2 vols.)
Gustave Le Rouge. *The Vampires of Mars The Dominion of the World* (w/Gustave Guitton) (4 vols.)
Jules Lermina. *Mysteryville; Panic in Paris; To-Ho and the Gold Destroyers; The Secret of Zippelius*
Jean-Marc & Randy Lofficier. *Edgar Allan Poe on Mars; The Katrina Protocol; Pacifica; Robonocchio; Tales of the Shadowmen 1-8*
Xavier Mauméjean. *The League of Heroes*
Joseph Méry. *The Tower of Destiny*
Hippolyte Mettais. *The Year 5865*
Louise Michel. *The Human Microbes; The New World*
José Moselli. *Illa's End*
John-Antoine Nau. *Enemy Force*
Marie Nizet. *Captain Vampire*
C. Nodier, A. Beraud & Toussaint-Merle. *Frankenstein*
Henri de Parville. *An Inhabitant of the Planet Mars*
Gaston de Pawlowski. *Journey to the Land of the 4th Dimension*
Georges Pellerin. *The World in 2000 Years*
Pierre Pelot. *The Child Who Walked on the Sky*
J. Polidori, C. Nodier, E. Scribe. *Lord Ruthven the Vampire*
P.-A. Ponson du Terrail. *The Vampire and the Devil's Son*
Henri de Régnier. *A Surfeit of Mirrors*
Maurice Renard. *The Blue Peril; Doctor Lerne; The Doctored Man; A Man Among the Microbes; The Master of Light*
Jean Richepin. *The Wing*
Albert Robida. *The Adventures of Saturnin Farandoul; The Clock of the Centuries; Chalet in the Sky*
J.-H. Rosny Aîné. *Helgvor of the Blue River; The Givreuse Enigma; The Mysterious Force; The Navigators of Space; Vamireh; The World of the Variants; The Young Vampire*
Marcel Rouff. *Journey to the Inverted World*
Han Ryner. *The Superhumans*

Brian Stableford. *The New Faust at the Tragicomique; The Empire of the Necromancers (The Shadow of Frankenstein; Frankenstein and the Vampire Countess; Frankenstein in London); Sherlock Holmes & The Vampires of Eternity; The Stones of Camelot; The Wayward Muse.* (anthologist) *The Germans on Venus; News from the Moon; The Supreme Progress; The World Above the World; Nemoville; Investigations of the Future*
Jacques Spitz. *The Eye of Purgatory*
Kurt Steiner. *Ortog*
Eugène Thébault. *Radio-Terror*
C.-F. Tiphaigne de La Roche. *Amilec*
Théo Varlet. *The Xenobiotic Invasion; Timeslip Troopers* (w/André Blandin); *The Martian Epic* (w/Octave Joncquel)
Paul Vibert. *The Mysterious Fluid*
Villiers de l'Isle-Adam. *The Scaffold; The Vampire Soul*
Philippe Ward. *Artahe*
Philippe Ward & Sylvie Miller. *The Song of Montségur*

MYSTERIES & THRILLERS

M. Allain & P. Souvestre. *The Daughter of Fantômas*
A. Anicet-Bourgeois, Lucien Dabril. *Rocambole*
A. Bernède. *Belphegor; Judex* (w/Louis Feuillade)
A. Bisson & G. Livet. *Nick Carter vs. Fantômas*
V. Darlay & H. de Gorsse. *Lupin vs. Holmes: The Stage Play*
Paul Féval. *Gentlemen of the Night; John Devil; The Black Coats ('Salem Street; The Invisible Weapon; The Parisian Jungle; The Companions of the Treasure; Heart of Steel; The Cadet Gang; The Sword-Swallower)*
Emile Gaboriau. *Monsieur Lecoq*
Steve Leadley. *Sherlock Holmes: The Circle of Blood*
Maurice Leblanc. *Arsène Lupin vs. Countess Cagliostro; Lupin vs. Holmes (The Blonde Phantom; The Hollow Needle); The Many Faces of Arsène Lupin*
Gaston Leroux. *Chéri-Bibi; The Phantom of the Opera; Rouletabille & the Mystery of the Yellow Room*
Richard Marsh. *The Complete Adventures of Judith Lee*
William Patrick Maynard. *The Terror of Fu Manchu; The Destiny of Fu Manchu*
Frank J. Morlock. *Sherlock Holmes: The Grand Horizontals; Sherlock Holmes vs Jack the Ripper*

Antonin Reschal. *The Adventures of Miss Boston*
P. de Wattyne & Y. Walter. *Sherlock Holmes vs. Fantômas*
David White. *Fantômas in America*

SCREENPLAYS

Mike Baron. *The Iron Triangle*
Emma Bull & Will Shetterly. *Nightspeeder; War for the Oaks*
Gerry Conway & Roy Thomas. *Doc Dynamo*
Steve Englehart. *Majorca*
James Hudnall. *The Devastator*
Jean-Marc & Randy Lofficier. *Royal Flush*
J.-M. & R. Lofficier & Marc Agapit. *Despair*
J.-M. & R. Lofficier & Joël Houssin. *City*
Andrew Paquette. *Peripheral Vision*
Robert L. Robinson, Jr. *Judex*
R. Thomas, J. Hendler & L. Sprague de Camp. *Rivers of Time*

NON-FICTION

Stephen R. Bissette. *Blur 1-5. Green Mountain Cinema 1; Teen Angels*
Win Scott Eckert. *Crossovers* (2 vols.)
Jean-Marc & Randy Lofficier. *Shadowmen* (2 vols.)
Randy Lofficier. *Over Here*

HEXAGON COMICS

Franco Frescura & Luciano Bernasconi. *Wampus*
Franco Frescura & Giorgio Trevisan. *CLASH*
L. Bernasconi, J.-M. Lofficier & Juan Roncagliolo Berger. *Phenix*
Claude Legrand, J.-M. Lofficier & L. Bernasconi. *Kabur*
Franco Oneta. *Zembla*
L. Buffolente, Lofficier & J.-J. Dzialowski. *Strangers: Homicron*
Danilo Grossi. *Strangers: Jaydee*
Claude Legrand & Luciano Bernasconi. *Strangers: Starlock*